Within The Precincts

Vol. III

by

Oliphant

Double 9 BOOKS

Within The Precincts
Vol. III
by Oliphant

ISBN: 978-93-71132-74-9

Published by

DOUBLE 9 BOOKS
2/13-B, Ansari Road
Daryaganj, New Delhi – 110002
info@double9books.com
www.double9books.com
Tel. 011-40042856

ABOUT THE AUTHOR

Margaret Oliphant was a Scottish author and historical writer who usually wrote under the name Mrs. Oliphant. She was born Margaret Oliphant Wilson on April 4, 1828, and died on June 20, 1897. She writes "domestic realism, the historical novel, and tales of the supernatural" as her short stories. Margaret Oliphant was born in Wallyford, near Musselburgh, East Lothian. She was the only daughter and youngest child still living of Margaret Oliphant (c. 1789–17 September 1854) and Francis W. Wilson, a clerk. We lived in Lasswade, Glasgow, and Liverpool when she was a child. In Wallyford, a street called Oliphant Gardens is named after her. As a girl, she was always trying new things with writing. Passages in the Life of Mrs. Margaret Maitland, her first book, came out in 1849. This was about the mostly successful Scottish Free Church movement, which was something her folks agreed with. Next came Caleb Field in 1851, the same year she met publisher William Blackwood in Edinburgh and was asked to write for Blackwood's Magazine. She did so for the rest of her life and wrote over 100 articles, including one that criticized Arthur Dimmesdale in Nathaniel Hawthorne's "The Scarlet Letter".

CONTENTS

CHAPTER XXXIII
LOTTIE'S SIDE OF THE QUESTION

Lottie made her way down the Slopes alone, with feelings which had greatly changed from those of a few minutes ago. How happy she had been! The hour that had passed under the falling leaves had been like paradise; but the portals of exit from paradise are perhaps never so sweet as those of entrance. Her coming away was with a sense of humiliation and shame. As she wound her way down her favourite by-road winding among the shrubs and trees, she could not help feeling that she was making her escape, as if from some guilty meeting, some clandestine rendezvous. In all her life Lottie had never known this sensation before. She had been shy, and had shrunk from the gaze of people who had stared at her, in admiration of her beauty or of her singing, but in her shyness there had always been the pride of innocence; and never before had she been afraid to meet any eye, or felt it necessary to steal away, to keep out of sight as if she were guilty. She had not done anything wrong, but yet she had all the feeling of having done something wrong—the desire to escape, the horror of detection. To some the secret meeting, the romance and mystery, would have been only an additional happiness, but Lottie, proud and frank and open-hearted, could not bear the very thought of doing anything of which she was ashamed. The sensation hurt and humiliated her. All had been very different *before*: to meet her lover unawares, yet not without intention, with a delightful element of chance in each encounter—to look out secretly for him, yet wonder innocently to find him—to let her steps be drawn here or there by a sense of his presence, with a fond pretence of avoiding him, a sweet certainty of meeting him—all these risks and hazards of emotion had been natural. But Lottie felt with a sudden jar of her nerves and mind that this ought not to continue so. She had felt a little wondering disappointment on the previous night when he had asked her to meet him again, without any suggestion that he should go to her, or make the new bond between them known. Even then there had been a faint jar, a sigh of unfulfilled expectation. But now their hurried parting, her own flight, the little panic lest they should be seen, and discovery follow, made Lottie's heart sick. How well she could imagine how this ought to have been! They ought not to have fled from each other, or been afraid of any man's eye. It ought not to have mattered whether the Signor or anyone suspected. Blushing and shy, yet with full faith in the sympathy of all who saw her, Lottie should have walked down the Dean's Walk with her betrothed: she should have avoided no one. She should have been shamefaced but not ashamed. What a difference between the two! all the difference that there is between the soft blush of happiness and the miserable burning of guilt. And this was what ought to have been. Half the misery of Lottie—as half the misery of all imaginative inexperienced women—arose from the pain and disappointment of feeling that those she loved did not come up to the ideal standard she had set up in her soul. She was disappointed, not so much because of the false position in which she herself was placed (for this, except instinctively, she had but little realised), but because Rollo was not doing, not yet, all that it seemed right for him to do. She would have forced and beaten (had she been able) Law into the fulfilment of his duty, she would even have made him generous to herself, not for the sake of herself, but that he should be a model of brotherhood, an example of all a true man ought to be; and if this was so in the case of her brother, how much more with her lover? If to be harsh as a tyrant or indifferent as a sultan, was the highest ideal of a man's conduct, how much happier many a poor creature would be! It seems a paradox to say so, but it is true enough; for the worst of all, in a woman's mind, is to feel that the wrong done to *her* is worse wrong to *him*, an infringement of the glory of the being whom she would fain see perfect. This, however, is a mystery beyond the comprehension of the crowd. Lottie was used to being disappointed with Law—was she fated to another disappointment more cruel and bitter? She did not ask herself the question, she would not have thought it even, much less said it for all the world; but secretly there was a wonder, a pang, a faintness of failure in her heart.

It is not without an effort, however, that the heart will permanently admit any such disappointment. As Lottie went her ways thus drooping, ashamed and discouraged, thinking of everything that had been done and that ought to have been done, there drifted vaguely across her mind a kind of picture of Rollo's meeting with her father, and what it would be. She had no sooner thought of this than a glow of alarm came over her face, bringing insensibly consolation to her mind. Rollo and her father! What would the Captain say to him? He would put on his grand air, in which even Lottie had no faith; he would exhibit himself in all his vain greatness, in all his self-importance, jaunty and fine, to his future son-in-law. He would give Lottie herself a word of commendation in passing, and he would spread himself forth before the stranger as if it was he whom Rollo wanted and cared for. Lottie's steps quickened out of the languid pace into which they had fallen, and her very forehead grew crimson as she realised that meeting. Thank heaven, it had not taken place yet! Rollo had been too wise, too kind, too delicate to humble his love by hurrying into the presence of the Captain, into the house where the Captain's new wife now reigned supreme. The new wife—she too would have a share in it, she would be called into counsel, she would give her advice in everything, and claim a right to interfere. Oh, Lottie thought, how foolish she had been! how much wiser was Rollo, no doubt casting about in his mind how it was best to be done, and pondering over it carefully to spare her pain. She felt herself enveloped in one blush from the crown of her head to the sole of her feet; but how sweet was that shame! It was she who was foolish, not he who had failed. Her cheeks burned with a penitential flush, but he was faultless. There was nothing in him to disappoint, but only the most delicate kindness, the tenderest care of her. How could she have thought otherwise? It was not possible that Rollo should like secret meetings, should fear discovery. In the first days of their acquaintance he had shown no reluctance to come to the humble little lodge. But now—his finer feeling shrank from it now—he wanted to take his love away from that desecrated place, not to shame her by prying into its ignoble mysteries. He was wiser, better, kinder than anyone. And she was ashamed of *herself*, not any longer of anything else, ashamed of her poor, mean, unworthy interpretation of him; and as happy in her new, changed consciousness of guilt, and penitence and self-disgust—as happy as if, after her downfall into earth, she had now safely got back into heaven.

By this time she had got out of the wooded Slopes, and over the stile, and into the steep thoroughfare at the foot of the Abbey walls, the pavement of St. Michael's Hill. Lottie did not feel that there was any harm in walking through the street alone, as Rollo thought there was. She wanted no attendant. A little bodyguard, invisible, but with a radiance going out from them which shone about her, attended upon her way—love and innocence and happiness, no longer with drooping heads but brave and sweet, a band invisible, guaranteeing their charge against all ills. As she went along the street with this shining retinue, there was nothing in all the world that could have harmed her; and nobody wanted to harm the girl—of whom, but that she was proud, no soul in St. Michael's had an unkind word to say. Everybody knew the domestic trouble that had come upon her, and all the town was sorry for Lottie—all the more that there was perhaps a human satisfaction in being sorry for one whose fault was that she was proud. She met Captain Temple as she entered the Abbey Gate. Many thoughts about her had been in the kind old man's heart all the morning, and it was partly to look for her, after vain walks about the Abbey Precincts, that he was turning his steps towards the town. He came up to her eagerly, taking her hand between his. He thought she must have been wandering out disconsolate, no matter where, to get away from the house which was no longer a fit home for one like her. He was so disturbed and anxious about her, that the shadow which was in his mind seemed to darken over Lottie, and cast a reflection of gloom upon her face. "You have been out early, my dear? Why did you not send for me to go with you? After matins I am always at your service," he said.

But there was none of the gloom which Captain Temple imagined in Lottie's face. She looked up at him out of the soft mist of her own musings with a smile. "I went out before matins," she said; "I have been out a long time. I had—something to do."

"My poor child! I fear you have been wandering, keeping out of the way," said the old Captain. Then another thought seized him. Had she begun already to serve the new wife and do her errands? "My dear," he said, "what have you been doing? you must not be too good—you must not forget yourself too much. Your duty to your father is one thing, but you must not let yourself be made use of now—you must recollect your own position, my dear."

"My position?" she looked up at him bewildered; for she was thinking only of Rollo, while he thought only of her father's wife.

"Yes, Lottie, my dear child, you have thought only of your duty hitherto, but you must not yield to every encroachment. You must not allow it to be supposed that you give up everything."

"Ah," said Lottie, lifting to him eyes which seemed to swim in a haze of light; "to give up everything would be so— I don't know what you mean," she added hastily, in a half-terrified tone. As for Captain Temple, he was quite bewildered, and did not know what to think.

"Need I explain, my dear, what I mean? There can be but one thing that all your friends are thinking of. This new relation, this new connection. I could not sleep all night for thinking of you, in the house with that woman. My poor child! and my wife too. You were the last thing we talked of at night, the first thing in the morning—"

"Ah," said Lottie again, coming back to reality with a long-drawn breath. "I was not thinking of her; but I understand you now."

Lottie had, however, some difficulty in thinking of *her*, even now; for one moment, being thus recalled to the idea, her countenance changed; but soon came back to its original expression. Her eyes were dewy and sweet—a suspicion of tears in them like the morning dew on flowers with the sunshine reflected in it, the long eyelashes moist, but the blue beneath as clear as a summer sky; and the corners of her mouth would run into curves of smiling unawares; her face was not the face of one upon whom the cares of the world were lying heavy, but of one to whom some new happiness had come. She was not thinking of what he was saying, but of something in her own mind. The kind old Captain could not tell what to think; he was alarmed, though he did not know why.

"Then it is not so bad," he said, "as you feared?"

"What is not so bad? Things at home? Oh, Captain Temple! But I try not to think about it," Lottie said hastily, with a quiver in her lip. She looked at him wistfully, with a sudden longing. "I wish—I wish—but it is better not to say anything."

"You may trust to me, my dear; whatever is in your heart I will never betray you; you may trust to me."

Lottie's eyes filled with tears as she looked at him, but she shook her head. They were not bitter tears, only a little bitter-sweet of happiness that wanted expression, but which she dared not reveal. If she could but have told him! If Rollo, failing her father, would but come and speak to this kind and true friend! But she shook her head. She was no longer free to say and do whatever pleased her out of her own heart. She must think of *him*; and while he did not speak, what could she say? She put out her hand to her old friend again with a little sudden artifice unlike Lottie. "I have been out all the morning," she said; "I must make haste and get back now."

"I am very glad you are not unhappy," said the old Captain, looking at her regretfully. He was not quite sincere. To tell the truth it gave him a shock to find that Lottie was not unhappy; how could she put up with such a companion, with such a fate? He went in to his wife, who had been watching furtively at the window while this conversation was going on, to talk it all over. Mrs. Temple was almost glad to find something below perfection in the girl about whom secretly she thought as much as her husband talked. "We have been thinking too much about it," she said; "if she can find the stepmother congenial, it will be better for her."

"Congenial! you are talking folly. How could she be congenial?" cried Captain Temple, with great heat, but he did not know what to make of it. He was disappointed in Lottie. When he had met her the day before she had been quivering with pain and shame, revolted and outraged, as it was right and natural she should be: but now it seemed to have passed altogether from her mind. He could not make it out. He was disappointed; he went on talking of this wonder all day long and shaking his white head.

As for Lottie, when she went home, she passed through the house, light and silent as a ghost, to her own little room, where, abstracted from everything else, she could live in the new little world of her own which had come out of the mists into such sudden and beautiful life. It was very unlike Lottie, but what more does the young soul want when the *vita nuova* has just begun, but such a possibility of self-abstraction and freedom to pursue its dreams? Rapt in these, she gave up her occupation, her charge, without a sigh. When she was called to table she came quite gently, and took no notice of anything that passed there, having enough in her own mind to keep her busy. Law was as much astonished as Captain Temple. He had thought that Lottie would not endure it for a day; but, thanks to that happy preoccupation, Lottie sailed serenely through these troubled waters for more than a week, during which she spent a considerable portion of her time on the Slopes, though the weather grew colder and colder every day, and the rest in her own room, in which she sat fireless, doing her accustomed needlework, her darnings and mendings, mechanically, while Polly remodelled the drawing-room, covering it up with crocheted antimacassars, and all the cheap and coarse devices of vulgar upholstery. While this was going on, she too was content to have Lottie out of the way. Polly pervaded the house with high-pitched voice and noisy step; and she filled it with savoury odours, giving the two men hot suppers, instead of poor Lottie's cold beef, which they had often found monotonous. The Captain now came in for this meal, which in former times he had rarely favoured; he spent the evenings chiefly at home, having not yet dropped out of the fervour of the honeymoon; and on the whole even Law was not sure that there was not something to be said for the new administration of the house. There was no cold beef—that was an improvement patent to the meanest capacity. As for Polly, nothing had yet occurred to mar her glory and happiness. She wore her blue silk every day, she walked gloriously about the streets in her orange-blossoms, pointed out by everybody as one of the ladies of the Abbey. She went to the afternoon service and sat in her privileged seat, and looked down with dignified sweetness upon "the girls" who were as she once was. She felt herself as a goddess, sitting there in the elevated place to which she had a right, and it seemed to her that to be a Chevalier's wife was as grand as to be a princess. But Polly did not soil her lips with so vulgar a word as wife. She called herself a Chevalier's lady, and her opinion of her class was great. "Chevalier means the same thing as knight, and, instead of being simple missis, I am sure we should all be My lady," Polly said, "if we had our rights." Even her husband laughed, but this did not change her opinion. It was ungrateful of the other Chevaliers' ladies that they took no notice of this new champion of their order. But for the moment Polly, in the elation of her success, did not mind this, and was content to wait for the recognition which sooner or later she felt would be sure to come.

This elation kept her from interfering with Lottie, whose self-absorbed life in her own room, and her exits and entrances, Mrs. Despard tolerated and seemed to accept as natural; she had so many things to occupy and to please her, that she could afford to let her step-daughter alone. And thus Lottie pursued for a little time that life out of nature to which she had been driven. She lived in those moments on the Slopes, and in the hours she spent at the Signor's piano, singing; and then brooded over these intervals of life in the silence. Her lessons had increased to three in the week, and these hours of so-called study were each like a drama of intense and curious interest. Rollo was always there—a fact which he explained to the Signor by his professional interest in the new singer, and which to Lottie required no explanation; and there too was her humble lover, young Purcell, who as she grew familiar with the sight of him, and showed no displeasure at his appearance, grew daily a little more courageous, sometimes daring to turn the leaves of the music, and even to speak to her. Mrs. O'Shaughnessy, who sat by, watching them all with lively but not extravagant interest, was the only one in the little party who was not more or less excited. As for Lottie, this lesson was the centre of all her life. If music be the food of love, love was the very inspiration of music to her; the two re-acted upon each other, raising her to such a height of primitive heroic passion as nobody near her divined—as nobody, indeed, except perhaps the Signor, with his Italian susceptibility, was capable of divining. He saw indeed with dissatisfaction, with an interest which was almost angry, that it was not art that moved her, and that the secret of the astonishing progress she made, was not in his instructions. What was it? The Signor was angry, for he felt no certainty that this wonderful progress was real. Something made her sing like an angel. What was it? not art. The natural qualities of her voice were not to be gainsayed; but the musician felt that the training under which she seemed to be advancing visibly, was all fictitious, and that it was something else that inspired her. But Rollo had no such enlightenment. He remarked with all the technicality of an amateur how her high notes gained in clearness, and her low notes in melody, at every new effort. It was wonderful; but then the Signor was a wonderful teacher, a wonderful accompanyist, and what so natural as that a creature of genius like this, should grow under his teaching like a flower? Though it was to him she sang, and though her love for him was her inspiration, Rollo was as unaware of this as old Pickering in the hall, who listened and shook his head, and decided in his heart that a woman with a voice like that was a deal too grand for Mr. John. "She's more like Jenny Lind than anything," old Pick said; and in this Mr. Ridsdale agreed, as he sat and listened, and thought over the means which should be employed to secure her success. As for young Purcell, he stood entranced and turned over the leaves of the music. Should he ever dare to speak to her again, to offer her his love, as he had once ventured to do,—she who seemed born to enthral the whole world? But then, the young fellow thought, who was there but he who had an 'ome to offer Lottie? He was the nobler of the two between whom she stood, the two men who loved her: all his thought was, that she being unhappy, poor, her father's house made wretched to her, he had an 'ome to offer her; whereas Rollo thought of nothing but of the success she must achieve in which he would have his share. In order to achieve that success Rollo had no mind to lend her even his name; but the idea that it was a thing certain, comforted him much in the consciousness of his own imprudent engagement, and gave a kind of sanction to his love. To marry a woman with such a faculty for earning money could not be called entirely imprudent. These were the calculations, generous and the reverse, which were made about her. Only Lottie herself made no calculations, but sang out of the fulness of her heart, and the delicate passion that possessed her; and the Signor stood and watched, dissatisfied, sympathetic, the only one that understood at all, though he but poorly, the high emotion and spring-tide of life which produced that flood of song.

In this highly-strained unnatural way, life went on amid this little group of people, few of whom were conscious of any volcano under their feet. It went on day by day, and they neither perceived the gathering rapidity of movement in the events, nor any other sign that to-day should not be as yesterday. Shortly after the explanation had taken place between Rollo and Lottie, Augusta Huntington, now Mrs. Daventry, arrived upon her first visit home. She was the Dean's only child, and naturally every honour was done to her. All the country round, everyone that was of sufficient importance to meet the Dean's daughter, was invited to hail her return. The Dean himself took the matter in hand to see that no one was overlooked. They would all like, he thought, to see Augusta, the princess royal of the reigning house; and Augusta was graciously pleased to like it too. One of these entertainments ended in a great musical party, to which all who had known Miss Huntington, all the singers in the madrigals and choruses of which she had been so fond, were asked. When Lottie's invitation came, there was a great thrill and commotion in Captain Despard's house. Lottie did not even suspect the feeling which had been roused on the subject when she took out her white muslin dress, now, alas, no longer so fresh as at first, and inspected it anxiously. It would do still with judicious ironing, but what must she do for ornaments, now that roses were no longer to be had? This troubled Lottie's mind greatly, though it may be thought a frivolous question, until a few hours before the time, when two different presents came for her, of flowers: one being a large and elaborate bouquet, the other a bunch of late roses, delicate, lovely, half-opened buds, which could only have come out of some conservatory. One of these was from Rollo, and who could doubt which it was? Who but he would have remembered her sole decoration, and found for her in winter those ornaments of June? What did she care who sent the other? She decked herself with her roses, in a glow of grateful tenderness, as proud as she was happy, to find herself thus provided by his delicate care and forethought. It did not even occur to Lottie to notice the dark looks that were thrown at her as she came downstairs all white and shining, and was wrapped by Law (always ostentatiously attentive to his sister in Polly's presence) in the borrowed glory of Mrs. O'Shaughnessy's great Indian shawl.

The party was large and crowded, and Lottie, all alone in it, was frightened and confused at first; but they were all very kind to her, she thought. Lady Caroline said, "How do you do, Miss Despard?" with something like a smile, and looked as if she might have given Lottie her hand, had not the girl been afraid; and Augusta, when she found her out, came forward with a welcome which was almost effusive. "I hear you have improved so much," she said, taking in at one glance all the particulars of Lottie's appearance, with a wondering question within herself where the roses came from, though she perceived at once that it was the same white muslin frock. And when Lottie sang, which the Signor managed she should do with great effect towards the close of the evening, Augusta rushed to her with great eyes of astonishment. "Where did you get all that voice?" she cried; "you did not have that voice when I went away." "I flatter myself it was I that found Miss Despard out," said Rollo, suffering himself to look at her, which hitherto he had only done when there was a shield of crowding groups between him and his cousin. Before this he had managed to make the evening sweet to Lottie by many a whispered word: but when he looked at her now, unawares, under Augusta's very eyes, with that fond look of proprietorship which is so unmistakable by the experienced, and to which Lottie responded shyly by a smile and blush, and conscious tremor of happiness, neither of them knew what a fatal moment it was. Augusta, looking on, suddenly woke up to the meaning of it, the meaning of Rollo's long stay at the Deanery, and various other wonders. She gave the pair but one look, and then she turned away. But Lottie did not see that anything strange had happened. She was so happy that even when Rollo too left her, her heart was touched and consoled by the kindly looks of the people whom she knew in the crowd, the ladies who had heard her sing before at the Deanery, and who were gracious to her, and Mr. Ashford who kept by her side and watched over her—"like a father," Lottie said to herself, with affectionate gratitude, such as might have become that impossible relationship. The Minor Canon did not leave her for the rest of the evening, and he it was who saw her home, waiting till the door was opened, and pressing kindly her trembling cold hand: for, she could not tell how, the end of the evening was depressing and discouraging, and the pleasure went all out of it when Rollo whispered to her in passing, "Take care, for heaven's sake, or Augusta will find us out!" Why should it matter so much to him that Augusta should find it out? Was not she more to him than Augusta? Lottie shrank within herself and trembled with a nervous chill. She was half grateful to, half angry with even Mr. Ashford. Why should he be so much more kind to her, so much more careful of her than the man who had promised her his love and perpetual care?

But even now when she stole in, shivering with the cold of disappointment and discouragement, through the dark house to her room Lottie did not know all that this evening had wrought. And she scarcely noticed the gloom on Polly's face, nor the strain of angry monologue which her father's wife gave vent to, next morning. Polly wondered what was the good of being a married lady, when a young unmarried girl that was nobody, was took such notice of, and her betters left at 'ome? Did people know no manners? gentlefolks! they called themselves gentlefolks, and behaved like that? If that was politeness, Polly thanked heaven it was not the kind as she had been taught. But the outburst came when Lottie, taking no notice, scarcely even hearing what was said, showed herself with her music in her hands going out to her lesson. Polly came out of her husband's room and planted herself defiantly in Lottie's way. "Where are you going again," she said, "Miss? where are you going again? is this to be always the way of it? Do you mean never to stay at home nor do anything to help nor make yourself agreeable? I declare it is enough to put a saint in a passion. But I won't put up with it, I can tell you. I did not come here to be treated like this, like the dirt under your feet."

Lottie was almost too much taken by surprise to speak. It was the first absolute shock of collision. "I am going for my lesson," she said.

"Your lesson!" cried Polly. "Oh my patience, oh my poor 'usband! that is the way his money goes—lessons for you and lessons for Law, and I don't know what! You ought to be ashamed of yourselves, you two. You ought to be making your living both of you, if you were honest, instead of living on your father as wants all he's got for himself. But you shan't go to any lesson if I can help it," she cried. "You'll stay at home and try and be of a little use, or you'll march off this very day, and find some one else to put up with you and your lessons. It shan't be me. I won't stand by and see my 'usband wronged. You'll ruin him between you, that's what you'll do; go back, Miss, and put down them books this moment. I won't have it, I tell you. I'll not see my 'usband eaten up by the likes of you."

Polly's diction suffered from her passion, and so did her appearance. Her face grew scarlet, her eyes flashed with fury. She put out her hand to push Lottie back, who shrank from her with a cry of dismay—

"Let me pass, please," said Lottie piteously. She could not quarrel with this woman, she could not even enter so much into conflict with her as to brush past her, and thus escape. She shrank with pain and horror from the excited creature in her way.

"It's you that will have to go back," said Polly, "not me. I'm the mistress of this house, you'll please to recollect, Miss Lottie. Your father's been a deal too good, he's let you do just what you pleased, but that's not my style. I begins as I mean to end. You shan't stay here, I tell you, whatever you may think, if you want to trample upon me, and eat up every penny he has. Go and take off your things this moment, and see if you can't be a little use in the house."

Lottie was struck dumb and could not tell what to say. She had not been cared for much in her life, but she had never been restrained, and the sensation was new to her. She did not know how to reply. "I do not wish to be in your way," she cried. "I shall not stay long nor trouble you long, but please do not interfere with me while I am here. I must go."

"And I say you shan't go!" said Polly, raising her voice after the manner of her kind, and stamping her foot upon the floor. "If you disobey me, I won't have you here not another day. I'll turn you out if it was twelve o'clock at night. I'll show you that I am mistress in my own house. Do you think I'm going to be outfaced by you, and treated like the dirt below your feet? Go and take off your things this moment, and try if you can't settle to a bit of work. Out of this house you shan't go, not a single step."

"I say, stand out of the way," said Law; he had come out of the dining-room with his hands in his pockets, having just finished his dinner. Law was not easily moved, but he had now made up his mind that he was on Lottie's side. "Don't give yourself airs to her. She is not of your sort," he said. "The governor may let you do many things, but not bully her. Look here, Polly, you'd better stand out of her way."

"And who are you, you lazy, useless lout, that dares to call me Polly?" she cried. "Polly, indeed! your father's wife, and far better than you. I'll make him put you to the door, too, you idle low fellow, spending your time with a pack of silly, dressing, useless girls—"

"I say, stop that," cried Law, growing red and seizing her suddenly by the arm; he stood upon no ceremony with Polly, though she was his father's wife; but he gave an uneasy alarmed glance at Lottie. "There's some one waiting for you outside," he cried. "Lottie, go."

She did not wait for any more. Trembling and horrified, she ran past and got out breathless, hastily closing the door behind her. The door had been open, and Mrs. O'Shaughnessy outside—drawing her skirts round her, physically and metaphorically, so as to avoid all pollution, yet listening to everything she could hear, was walking up and down the pavement. "Me poor child!" the good Irishwoman said, half sorry, half delighted to hear the first of the scandal. "Already! has it come to this? Me heart is sore for ye, Lottie me dear!"

CHAPTER XXXIV
A CRISIS

Lottie scarcely knew how she got through that afternoon. Rollo presented himself for but a moment at the Signor's, in great concern that he could not stay, and begging a hundred pardons with his eyes, which he could not put into words. Lady Caroline and Augusta had made an engagement for him from which he could not get free. "At the elm-tree!" he whispered in the only moment when he could approach Lottie. Her heart, which was beating still with the mingled anger, and wonder, and fright of her late encounter, sank within her. She could only look at him with a glance which was half appeal and half despair. And when he went away the day seemed to close in, the clouds to gather over the very window by which she was standing, and heaven and earth to fail her. Rollo's place was taken by a spectator whose sympathy was more disinterested than that of Rollo, and his pity more tender; but what was that to Lottie, who wanted only the one man whom she loved, not any other? What a saving of trouble and pain there would be in this world if the sympathy of one did as well as that of another! There was poor Purcell turning over the music, gazing at her with timid eyes full of devotion, and longing to have the courage and the opportunity to offer her again that 'ome which poor Lottie so much wanted, which seemed opened to her nowhere else in the whole world. And on the other side stood Mr. Ashford without any such definite intention as Purcell, without any perception as yet of anything in himself but extreme "interest in," and compassion for, this solitary creature, but roused to the depths of his heart by the sight of her, anxious to do anything that could give her consolation, and ready to stand by her against all the world. The Minor Canon had been passing when that scene took place in the hall of Captain Despard's house with its open door. He had heard Polly's loud voice, and he had seen Law rush out, putting on his hat, and flushed with unusual feeling. "I don't mind what she says to me as long as she keeps off Lottie!" the young man had said; and careless as Law was, the tears had come to his eyes, and he had burst forth, "My poor Lottie! what is she to do?" Mr. Ashford's heart had been wrung by this outcry. What could he do?—he was helpless—an unmarried man; of what use could he ever be to a beautiful, friendless girl? He felt how impotent he was with an impatience and distress which did not lessen that certainty. He could do nothing for her, and yet he could not be content to do nothing. This was why he came to the Signor's, sitting down behind backs beside Mrs. O'Shaughnessy, who distracted him by much pantomimic distress, shaking her head and lifting up her hands and eyes, and would fain have whispered to him all the time of Lottie's singing had not the Signor sternly interfered. ("Sure these musical folks they're as big tyrants as the Rooshians themselves," Mrs. O'Shaughnessy said indignantly.) This was all the Minor Canon could do—to come and stand by the lonely girl, though no one but himself knew what his meaning was. It could not be any help to Lottie, who was not even conscious of it. Perhaps, after all, the sole good in it was to himself.

Lottie had never sung so little well. She did not sing badly. She took trouble; the Signor felt she tried to do her best, to work at it, to occupy herself with the music by way of getting rid of things more urgent which would press themselves upon her. In short, for the time Lottie applied herself to it with some faint conception of the purposes of art. To have recourse to art as an opiate against the pangs of the inner being, as an escape from the harms of life, is perhaps not the best way of coming at it, but the Signor knew that this was one of the most beaten ways towards that temple which to him enshrined everything that was best in the world. It was, perhaps, the only way in which Lottie was likely to get at it, and he saw and understood the effort. But it could not be said that the effort was very successful. The others, who were thinking only of her, felt that Lottie did not do so well as usual. She was not in voice, Purcell said to himself; and to the Minor Canon it seemed very natural that after the scene which she had just gone through poor Lottie should have but little heart for her work. It was easily explained. The Signor, however, who knew nothing of the circumstances, came to the most true conclusion. The agitation of that episode with Polly would not have harmed her singing, however it might have troubled herself, had Lottie's citadel of personal happiness been untouched. But the flag was lowered from that donjon, the sovereign was absent. There was no inspiration left in the dull and narrowed world where Lottie found herself left. Her first opening of vigorous independent life had been taken from her, and for the first time the life of visionary passion and enthusiasm was laid low. She did not give in. She made a brave effort, stilling her excited nerves, commanding her depressed heart. The Signor himself was more excited than he had been by all the previous easy triumphs of her inspiration. Now was the test of what she had in her. Happiness dies, love fails, but art is for ever. Could she rise to the height of this principle, or would she drop upon the threshold of the sacred place incapable of answering to the guidance of art alone? Never before had he felt the same anxious interest in Lottie. He thought she was groping for that guidance, though without knowing it, in mere instinct of pain to find something that would not fail her. She did not rise so high as she had done under the other leading; but to the Signor this seemed to be in reality Lottie's first step, though she did not know it, on the rugged ascent which is the artist's way of life. Strait is the path and narrow is the way in that, as in all excellence. The Signor praised her more than he had ever praised her before, to the surprise of the lookers-on; the generous enthusiasm of the artist glowed in him. If he could, he would have helped her over the roughness of the way, just as the Minor Canon, longing and pitiful, would have helped her if he could, over the roughness of life. But the one man was still more powerless than the other to smooth her path. Here it was not sex, nor circumstances, which were in fault, but the rigid principles of art, which are less yielding than rocks; every step, however painful, in that thorny way the neophyte must tread for herself. The Signor knew it; but the more his beginner stumbled, the more eager was he to cheer her on.

"I am afraid I sang very badly," Lottie said, coming out with Mrs. O'Shaughnessy and the Minor Canon, who went along with them he scarcely knew why. He could do nothing for the girl, but he did not like to leave her—to seem (to himself) to desert her. Only himself was in the least degree aware that he was standing by Lottie in her trouble.

"Me child, you all think a deal too much about it. It was neither better nor worse; that's what I don't like in all your singing. It may be fine music, but it's always the same thing over and over. If it was a tune that a body could catch—but it's little good the best tune would have been to me this day. I didn't hear you, Lottie, for thinking what was to become of you. What will ye do? Will you never mind, but go back? Sure you've a right to your father's house whatever happens, and I wouldn't be driven away at the first word. There is nothing would please her so well. I'd go back!"

"Oh, don't say any more!" cried Lottie with a movement of sudden pride. But when she caught the pitying look of the Minor Canon her heart melted. "Mr. Ashford will not be angry because I don't like to speak of it," she said, raising her eyes to him. "He knows that things are not—not very happy—at home."

Then Mr. Ashford awoke to the thought that he might be intruding upon her. He took leave of the ladies hurriedly. But when she had given him her hand, he stood holding it for a minute. "I begin to like Law very much," he said. To feel that this was the way in which he could give her most pleasure was a delicate instinct, but it was not such a pleasure as it would have been a month ago. Lottie did not speak, but a gleam of satisfaction rose in her eyes. "If there is anything I can do," he said faltering, "to be of use—"

What could he do? Nothing? He knew that, and so did she. It was only to himself that this was a consolation, he said to himself when they were gone. He went away to his comfortable house; and she, slim and light, turned to the other side of the Abbey, with Mrs. O'Shaughnessy, with nowhere in the world to go to. Was that so? was it really so? But still he, with that house of his, a better home than the one which young Purcell was so eager to offer her, what could he do? Nothing; unless it were one thing which had not before entered his thoughts, and now, when it had got in, startled him so, that, middle-aged as he was, he felt his countenance turn fiery red, and went off at a tremendous pace, as if he had miles to go. He had only a very little way to go before he reached his own door, and yet he had travelled more than miles between that and the dwelling of the Signor.

As for Lottie, she went home with Mrs. O'Shaughnessy, not knowing what she was to do after. The elm-tree—that was the only place in the world that seemed quite clear to her. For a moment, in the sickness of her disappointment to see Rollo abandon her, she had said to herself that she would not go; but soon a longing to tell him her trouble came upon her. After the Abbey bells had roused all the echoes, and the usual congregation had come from all quarters for the evening service, she left Mrs. O'Shaughnessy, and went slowly towards the Slopes. It was still early, and the wintry afternoon was cold. There was an east wind blowing, parching the landscape, and turning all its living tints into lines of grey. Lottie was not very warmly clothed. She had her merino gown and little cloth jacket, very plain garments, not like the furs in which Augusta had come home; but, then, Lottie was not used to living like Augusta, and perhaps her thinner wrap kept her as warm. She went up the Dean's Walk languidly, knowing that it was too early, but unable to rest. She would have to go home after all, to steal in and hide herself in her room, for this night at least; but, after that, what was she to do? The O'Shaughnessys had not a room to give her. She had no relations whom she might go to; what was to become of her? When she got to the elm-tree there was nobody there. She had known it was too early. She sat down and thought, but what could thinking do? What could she make of it? She looked over the wide landscape which had so often stilled and consoled her, but it was all dead and unresponsive, dried up by that east wind; the earth and the sky, and even the horizon on which they met, all drawn in pale outlines of grey. Her face was blank and pale, like the landscape, when the lover for whom she was waiting appeared. The wind, which was so cold, had driven everybody else away. They had it all to themselves, this chilly wintry landscape, the shadowy trees, with a few ragged garments of yellow or faded brown still clinging to them. Rollo came up breathless, his feet ringing upon the winding path. He came and placed himself beside her, with a thousand apologies that she should have had to wait. "It was a trick of Augusta's," he said; "I am sure she suspects something." Lottie felt that this repeated suggestion that someone suspected ought not to be made to her. But her paleness and sadness roused Rollo to the most hearty concern. "Something has happened," he said; "I can see it, darling, in your eyes. Tell me what it is. Have not I a right to know everything?" Indeed he was so anxious and so tender that Lottie forgot all about offence and her disappointment, and everything that was painful. Who had she beside to relieve her burdened heart to, to lean upon in her trouble? She told him what had happened, feeling that with every word she uttered her load was being lightened. Oh! how good it is to be able to say forth everything, to tell someone to whom all that happens to you is interesting! As she told Polly's insults, even Polly herself seemed to grow more supportable. Rollo listened to every word with anxious interest, with excitement, and indignation and grief. He held her closer to him, saying, "My poor darling, my poor Lottie!" with outbursts of rage and tender pity. Lottie's heart grew lighter and lighter as she went on. He seemed to her to be taking it all on his shoulders, the whole of the burden. His eyes shone with love and indignation. It was not a thing which could be borne; she must not bear it, he would not allow her to bear it, he cried. Finally, a great excitement seemed to get possession of him all at once. A sudden impulse seized upon him. He held her closer than ever, with a sudden tightening of his clasp, and hasty resolution. "Lottie!" he cried; and she could feel his heart suddenly leap into wild beating, and looked up trembling and expectant, sure that he had found some way of deliverance. "Lottie, my love! you must not put up with this another day. You must come away at once. Why not this very night? I could not rest and think you were bearing such indignity. You must be brave, and trust yourself to me. You will not be afraid, my darling, to trust yourself to me?"

"To-night!" she said, with a cry of answering excitement, alarm, and wonder.

"Why not to-night?" he cried, with more and more energy. "I know a place where I could take you. A quiet, safe place, with people to take care of you, who would not suffer you to be annoyed even when I was not there myself to watch over you. Lottie, dearest, you would not be afraid to trust yourself to me?"

"No, Rollo, why should I be afraid?—but—" The suddenness of this prospect of deliverance, which she did not understand, took away Lottie's breath.

"But—there are no buts. You would be taken care of as if you were in a palace. You would have everything to make your life pleasant. You could work at your music—"

"Ah!" she said, interrupting him; his excitement roused no alarm in her mind. She was incapable of understanding any meaning in him that was inconsistent with honour. "Would it be so necessary to think of the music?" she said. It seemed to her that for Rollo Ridsdale's wife it need not be any longer a point essential. A host of other duties, more sweet, more homely, came before her dazzled eyes.

"Above all things!" he said, with a sudden panic, "without that what would you—how could I?—"—the suggestion was insupportable—"but we can discuss this after," he said. "Lottie, my Lottie, listen! Trust yourself to me—let me take you away out of all this misery into happiness. Such happiness! I scarcely can put it into words. Why should you have another day of persecution, when you can be free, if you will, this very night?"

His countenance seemed aflame as he bent towards her in the wintry twilight; she could feel the tumultuous beating of his heart. It was no premeditated villany, but a real impulse, acted upon, without any pause for thought, with that sudden and impassioned energy which is often more subtle than the craftiest calculation. Even while his heart beat thus wildly with awakened passion, Rollo answered the feeble resistance of his conscience by asking himself what harm could it do her? it would not interfere with her career. As for Lottie, she raised herself up within his arm and threw back her head and looked at him, not shrinking from him nor showing any horror of the suggestion. There was a pause—only for a moment, but it felt like half-an-hour, while wild excitement, love, and terror coursed through his veins. Surely she understood him, and was not alarmed? If she had understood him and flung away from him in outraged virtue, Rollo would have been abject in guilt and penitence. For the moment, however, though his heart beat with alarm, there was a sense of coming triumph in all his being.

Lottie raised her drooping shoulders, she threw back her head and looked at him, into the glowing face that was so close to her. Her heart had given one answering leap of excitement, but was not beating like his. At that moment, so tremendous to him, it was not passion, but reflection, that was in her eyes.

"Let me think—let us think," she said. "Oh, Rollo! it is a great temptation. To go away, to be safe with you—"

"My darling, my own darling! you shall never have cause to fear, never to doubt me; my love will be as steady, as true—" So high had the excitement of suspense grown, that he had scarcely breath to get out the words.

"Do you think I doubt that?" she said, her voice sounding so calm, so soft to his excited ear. "That is not the question; there are so many other things to think of. If you will not think for yourself, I must think for you. Oh, Rollo, no! I don't see how it could be. Listen to me; you are too eager, oh! thank you, dear Rollo, too fond of me, to take everything into consideration—but *I* must. Rollo! no, no; it would never do; how could it ever do, if you will only think? Supposing even that it did not matter for me, how could you marry your wife from any place but her home? It would not be creditable," said Lottie, shaking her head with all the gentle superiority of reason, "it would not be right or becoming for you."

His arm relaxed round her; he tried to say something, but it died away in his throat. For the moment the man was conscious of nothing but a positive pang of gratitude for a danger escaped; he was safe, but he scarcely dared breathe. Had she understood him as he meant her to understand him, what vengeance would have flashed upon him, what thunderbolt scathed him! But for very terror he would have shrunk and hid his face now in the trembling of the catastrophe escaped.

"More than that, even," said Lottie, going on all unaware; "I have nothing, you know; and how could I take money—*money to live upon*—from *you*!—till I was married to you? No! it is impossible, impossible, Rollo. Oh! thank you, thank you a thousand times for having thought more of me than of anything else; but you see, don't you see, how impossible it is? I will never forget," said the girl softly, drawing a little closer to him who had fallen away from her in the strange tumult of failure—yet deliverance—which took all strength from him, "I will never forget that you were ready to forget everything that was reasonable, everything that was sensible, and even your own credit, for me!"

Another pause, but this time indescribable. In her bosom gratitude, tender love, and that sweet sense of calmer judgment, of reason less influenced by passion than it would be fitting or right for his to be, which a woman loves to feel within herself—her modest prerogative in the supreme moment; in his a tumult of love, disappointment, relief, horror of himself, anger and shame, and the thrill of a hairbreadth escape. He could not say a word; what he had done seemed incredible to him. The most tremendous denunciation would not have humbled him as did her unconsciousness. He had made her the most villainous proposal, and she had not even known what it meant; to her it had seemed all generosity, love, and honour. His arm dropped from around her, he had no force to hold her, and some inarticulate exclamation—he could not tell what—sounded hoarsely in utter confusion and shame in his throat.

"You are not angry?" she said, almost wooing him in her turn. "Rollo, it is not that I do not trust you, you know; who should I trust but you? If that were all, I would put my hand in yours; you should take me wherever you pleased. But then there are the other things to be considered. And, Rollo, don't be angry," she said, drawing his arm within hers, "I can bear anything now. After talking to you, after feeling your sympathy, I can bear anything. What do I care for a woman like that? Of course I knew," said Lottie, with tears in her eyes, "that you did feel for me, that you thought of me, that you were always on my side. But one wants to have it said over again to make assurance sure. Now I can bear anything, now I can go home—though it is not much home—and wait, till you come and fetch me, Rollo, openly, in the light, in the day."

Here, because she was so happy, Lottie put her hands up to her face and laid those hands upon his shoulder and cried there in such a heavenly folly of pain and blessedness as words could not describe. That he should not claim her at once, that was a pain to her; and to think of that strange, horrible house to which she must creep back, that was pain which no happiness could altogether drive out of her thoughts. But yet, how happy she was! What did it matter if for the moment her heart was often sore? A little while and all would be well; a little while and she would be delivered out of all these troubles. It was only a question of courage, of endurance, of fortitude, and patience; and Lottie had got back her inspiration, and felt herself capable of bearing anything, everything, with a stout heart. But Rollo had neither recovered his speech nor his self-possession; shame and anger were in his heart. He had not been found out, but the very awe of escape was mingled with intolerable anger; anger no doubt chiefly against himself, but also a little against her, though why he could not have said. The unconsciousness of her innocence, which had impressed him so deeply at first and confounded all his calculations, began to irritate him. How was it possible she did not understand? was there stupidity as well as innocence in it? Most people would have had no difficulty in understanding, it would have been as clear as noonday—or, rather, as clear as gaslight; as evident as any "intention" could be. He could not bear this superiority, this obtuseness of believing; it offended him, notwithstanding that he had made by it what he felt to be the greatest escape of his life.

They parted after this not with the same enthusiasm on Rollo's part as that which existed on Lottie's. She was chilled, too, thinking he was angry with her for not yielding to his desire; and this overcast her happiness, but not seriously. They stole down by the side of the Abbey, in the shadow—Lottie talking, Rollo silent. When they came within sight of the cloister gate and the line of the lodges opposite, Lottie withdrew her hand from his arm. The road looked empty and dark; but who could tell what spectator might suddenly appear? She took his *rôle* in the eagerness of her heart to make up to him for any vexation her refusal might have given. "Don't come any further," she whispered; "let us part here; someone might see us." In her eagerness to make up to him for her own unkindness, she allowed the necessity for keeping that secret—though to think of it as a secret had wounded her before. Nevertheless, when he took her at her word and left her, Lottie, like the fanciful girl she was, felt a pang of disappointment and painfully realised her own desolateness, the dismal return all alone to the house out of which every quality of kindness had gone. Her heart sank, and with reluctant, lingering steps she came out of the Abbey shadow and began to cross the Dean's Walk, her forlorn figure moving slowly against the white line of the road and the grey of the wintry sky.

Someone was standing at the door as she came in sight of her father's house. It was Captain Despard himself, looking out. "Is that you, Lottie?" he called out, peering into the gloom. "Come in, come in; where have you been? You must not stay out again, making everybody anxious." Then he came out a step or two from his door and spoke in a whisper: "You know what a woman's tongue is," he said; "they have a great deal to answer for; but when they get excited, what can stop them? You must try not to pay any attention; be sensible, and don't mind—no more than I do," Captain Despard said.

CHAPTER XXXV
FAMILY DUTY: ACCORDING TO MRS. DESPARD

There are some victories which feel very much like defeats. When Polly had scattered her adversaries on every side, driven forth Lottie and got rid of Law, and silenced Captain Despard—who sat in his room and heard everything but thought it wisest not to interfere—she retired upstairs to her drawing-room and celebrated her triumph by shedding torrents of tears. She had intended to make everybody very wretched, and she had done so; supposing, perhaps (though she did not really know what her motive was), that some pleasure would come to herself out of the discomfiture of the others. But pleasure rarely comes by that means, and when she had thus chased everybody out of her way, Polly threw herself down and burst forth into angry sobs and tears. It is not to be supposed that Captain Despard entertained any romantic illusions about his bride; he knew very well what Polly was. He had, as facts proved, been sufficiently fond of her to marry her, but he did not expect of her more than Polly could give, nor was he shocked to find that she had a temper and could give violent utterance to its vagaries; all this he had known very well before. Knowing it, however, he thought it wise to keep out of the way and not mix himself up in a fray with which evidently he had nothing to do. Had she gone a step further with Lottie it is possible that he might have interfered, for, after all, Lottie was his child; and though he might himself be hard upon her at times, there is generally a mingled sentiment of family pride and feeling which makes us unwilling to allow one who belongs to us to be roughly treated by a stranger. But when Law put himself in the breach, his father sat close and took no notice; he did not feel impelled to turn his wife's batteries upon himself out of consideration for Law. Nor did it make any impression upon the Captain when he heard her angry sobs overhead. "She will come to if she is left to herself," he said, and he did not allow himself to be disturbed. Polly, in her passion, threw herself on the carpet, leaning her head upon a chair. She had changed the room after her own fashion. She had lined the curtains with pink muslin, and fastened her crochet-work upon the chairs with bows of pink ribbon; she had covered the old piano with a painted cover, and adorned it with vases and paper flowers. She had made the faded little room which had seemed a fit home enough, in its grey and worn humility, for Lottie's young beauty, into something that looked very much like a dressmaker's ante-room, or that terrible chamber, "handsomely fitted up with toilet requisites," where the victims of the photographic camera prepare for the ordeal. But the loveliness of her handiwork did not console Polly; she got no comfort out of the pink bows, nor even from the antimacassars—a point in which Lottie's room was painfully deficient. She flung herself upon the carpet and sobbed. What was the use of being a lady, a Chevalier's wife, and living here in the heart of the Abbey, if no one called upon her or took any notice of her? Polly was not of a patient nature; it did not occur to her even that there was still time for the courtesies she had set her heart upon gaining. She had looked every day for some one to come, and no one had ever come; no one had made any advances to her at the Abbey, which was the only place in which she could assert her position as a lady and a Chevalier's wife. Even Mrs. O'Shaughnessy, who had risen from the ranks, who lived next door, who was not a bit better, nay, who was much less good than Polly to begin with (for what is a trooper's wife? and she had been nothing but a trooper's wife)—even Mrs. O'Shaughnessy had passed the door as if she did not see it, and had waited outside till Miss Lottie came to her. Polly's dreams had been very different. She had seen herself in imagination the admired of all admirers; she was by far the youngest of all the Chevaliers' wives, and the gentlemen, at least, she was sure would rally round her. Women might be spiteful, but men always did justice to a woman when she was handsome and young. Was not that written in all the records? She expected that the ladies would be spiteful—*that* would be indeed a part of her triumph. They would be jealous of her superior attractions, of her youth, of her husband's adoration of her; the old things would be in a flutter of alarm lest their old men should come within her influence. But Polly had felt pretty sure that the old gentlemen would admire her and rally round her. To make the women envious and the men enthusiastic, was not that always the way? certainly such was the course of events in the *Family Herald*. The heroine might have one friend devoted to her fortunes, a confidant more admiring, more faithful even than her lover; but all the rest of womankind was leagued against her. And so it had been in most of the novels Polly had read. But that neither men nor women should take any notice, that was a thing for which she was not prepared, and which she declared to herself she would not bear.

She had seen enough already from her windows to make her furious. She had seen Mrs. O'Shaughnessy ostentatiously waiting for Lottie, walking up and down outside, making signs to the girl upstairs. She had seen Captain Temple pass and repass, looking up at the same window. She had seen the greetings that met Lottie wherever she appeared. The Chevaliers and their wives had not always looked upon Miss Despard with such favourable eyes. They had thought her proud, and they had resented her pride; but now that Lottie was in trouble it was round her they had all rallied. It was the party at the Deanery, however, which had been the last drop in Polly's cup. How was she to know that on the highest elevation she could reach as the lady of a Chevalier, she was still beneath the notice of Lady Caroline, and as far as ever from the heaven of the highest society? Polly did not know. The elevation to which she herself had risen was so immense in her own consciousness that there seemed no distinction of ranks above her. She thought, as Lottie had once thought, though from a different point of view, that gentlefolks were all one; that a gentleman's wife, if not so rich or so grand, was still on a level with Lady Caroline herself, and within the circle which encompassed the Queen. "You can't be no better than a gentleman," Polly said to herself. You might, it was true, be a lord, which some people thought better, but even a lord was scarcely above an officer. All this glorious ambition, however, what was it going to end in? She watched the carriages going to the Deanery, and with still more furious feelings she watched Lottie in her white dress crossing the Dean's Walk. And she left at home, at the window, neglected, left out, though she was Mrs. Despard, and the other nobody! Was it possible that it might be better even to be a dressmaker, forewoman in the workroom, acknowledged to have the best eye for cutting out, and to be the quickest worker of the lot, superior so far among her equals—than to be ignored and neglected and treated as the dust under their feet by a set of poor gentlefolks? Polly felt that she must wreak her vengeance on somebody.

When she had got her fit of crying over accordingly, she jumped up to her feet and hurried to her room to put on her "things." It was her "best things" that she put on. Indeed, Polly had been wearing her best things every day with an extravagance which rather touched her conscience, though it delighted her fancy. She made herself very fine indeed that wintry afternoon, and pattered downstairs upon a pair of high heels which were more splendid than comfortable, and burst into the little room where Captain Despard sat attentive to all these sounds, and wondering what was coming next. Few people realise the advantage of a silly wife to a man who is not over wise. The Captain, though he had a high opinion of himself, was aware at the bottom of his heart that other people scarcely shared that sentiment. And to have a wife whom he was fond of, and whose acquisition flattered his vanity, and who was unmistakably, though clever enough, less clever, less instructed, than he was, gave him a sense of superiority which was very pleasant to him. He looked upon her follies with much more indulgence than he had ever felt for Lottie, who did not give him the same consolation.

"Well, what is it now?" he said, with a smile.

"I want you to come out with me," Polly said. "I want to buy some things. My old muff is shabby, I couldn't wear it in the Abbey. Though they're a set of old frights and frumps, I don't wish your wife to be looked down upon by them, Harry. I can see them looking at all my things, counting up what everything costs, and whispering behind my back. That old Mrs. Jones has trimmed her bonnet exactly like mine, though she looks as if she was too grand to see me. They ain't above copying me, that's one thing."

"No wonder," said the admiring husband; "for it is long since anything so young and so handsome has been among them before. Don't they wish they could copy your face as well as your bonnet! that's all."

"Oh, get along!" said Polly, well pleased; "you're always flattering. Come and buy me a muff. I don't know what kind to get. Grebe is sweetly pretty and ermine is delicious, but sealskin, perhaps, is the most genteel; that always looks lady-like. Did you see Mrs. Daventry go by in her carriage? Ah!" Polly sighed; how could she help it? She was very fine in her blue silk, but Augusta was finer. "She has just come from France, you know, and then, of course, they are rich. She had on a velvet with sable *that* deep—! Ah! it's hard to see folks that are no better than you with things that are so much better," cried Polly; "but, after all, though velvet and sable are very nice, give me sealskin—that's always lady-like. A sealskin jacket!—if I had that, I don't think there is anything more I should wish for in the world."

"Are they very dear?" said the Captain, with a sudden fit of liberality. He had a native love of buying, which is very general with impecunious persons, and at present was in a prodigal mood.

"Dear! Oh, not for the good they are," said Polly. "You never want another winter mantle all your life. You're set up. That makes them cheap in the end; but they cost a deal of money. I haven't seen nobody with one in all the Abbey, except the Canon's ladies."

"Then you shall have one!" said Captain Despard. He looked like a prince, Polly thought, as he stood there glowing with generous purpose. The sound of the "O—Oh!" with which she received the offer rang through the Lodges. Such a shriek of pleasure had not been heard there since there had been Chevaliers in St. Michael's. They went out together, all beaming, arm in arm, the bride clinging fondly to her husband, the Captain looking down with delighted protection upon his bride. This sight, which is so pretty in some cases, and calls forth, if much amusement, often a great deal of sympathy, roused anything but friendly feelings in the Lodges, where the good people were getting ready for the afternoon service. Old fool was the best name they had for the bridegroom, though he was not very old; and Polly was a grievance which the ladies could not tolerate. They looked after her from their windows with feelings which were far from Christian. It was a thing they ought not to have been exposed to. There should have been an appeal to the Queen, if the gentlemen had the least energy. "But even the Queen, bless her! could not keep a man from marrying," the Warden said, deprecatingly. He did not like it any more than they did; but it is only when you are yourself of the executive that you know the difficulties of action; that is why the ladies are such critics—they have not got it to do.

Captain and Mrs. Captain Despard (Polly had got beautiful glazed cards printed stiff and strong with this title upon them) walked down to the best shop in St. Michael's, which is a very good shop indeed; and there they bought a *beautiful sealskin*. Impossible to tell the pride, the happiness, the glory with which Polly acquired this new possession. She had not expected it. These were the days when sealskins were still a hope, a desire, an aspiration to the female mind, a property which elevated its possessor, and identified her among her peers. "That lady with the sealskin," who would think of pointing out anybody by so general a description now? are they not even going out of fashion? But Polly, for one, could not realise the possibility that such a thing could ever happen. And she had not anticipated such a bliss; the happiness was doubled by being unforeseen. This, indeed, was a proof of the blessedness of being a married lady, of having bettered herself, of having married a gentleman. Her mind was in a confusion of delight. Nevertheless she did not forget that she had come out with another and quite distinct purpose. The fact that she had herself been so fortunate did not turn her from her mission. Was it not more her duty than ever to do everything that could be done for her husband's family? When she had decided upon her sealskin, Polly began to shiver. She said, "It is a very cold day. I don't know why it should be so cold so early in the year. Don't you think it is very cold, Harry? I have come out without any wrap. Do you know I think I will put the sealskin *on*." Why should not she? The proprietor of the shop accomplished the sale with a pang. He knew Captain Despard well enough and he knew Polly, and he trembled when he thought of his bill. But what could he be but civil? He put it on for her—though how any ordinary sealskin could have covered a bosom so swelling with pride and bliss it is hard to say. And the pair went out together as they came in, except that one was almost speechless with the proud consciousness of drawing all eyes. "It is not the appearance," said Polly, "but it *is* so deliciously warm; there never was anything like it. And now I am set up. I shall not cost you any more for a winter cloak, not for years and years." "I thought you said it was to last for ever," said the Captain, equally delighted. They promenaded all the way down St. Michael's Hill, the admired of all beholders. If the remarks that were made were not precisely such as Polly hoped, still there was no doubt that remarks were made by everybody, and that the sealskin had all the honour it deserved. Sometimes, indeed, there would be a bitter in the sweet, as when the Captain took off his hat with jaunty grace to some lady whom he knew. "Who is that?" Polly would ask sharply; but the ladies all hurried by, and never stopped to be introduced; and no man took off his hat to Polly. Even against this, however, the happiness that wrapped her round defended Mrs. Despard. And how the people stared!—people who had seen her going up and down with a little bundle of patterns on her way to her work, on her way to try on a dress—people in the shops, who had been her equals if not her superiors—to see them gazing out at her with big eyes, at her fine sealskin and her fine husband, that comforted her soul. She walked slowly, getting the full good of her triumph. But when she had got to the foot of the hill she dismissed her escort. "Now you may go," she said; "you always had plenty to do in the old days. I don't want you to say *I* tie you to my apron-string. You may go now."

"This is a pretty way to dismiss your husband," said Captain Despard; "and where are you going, may I ask, that you send me away?"

"Oh, I will tell you fast enough. I am not going anywhere you can disapprove of. I am going to see the girls," said Polly, "that is all."

"The girls! My love, you must recollect," said Captain Despard with dignity, "that the girls, as you call them, are not fit companions for you."

"You may trust me to know my place," said Polly, "and to keep them in theirs. I should think you may trust *me*."

Fortified by this assurance, the Captain left his lovely bride. He turned back to kiss his hand to her when he was half way up the hill, prolonging the sweet sorrow of the parting, and Polly blew him a kiss with infantine grace. It was "as good as a play." "Lord, what fools they are!" said the fishmonger on the hill, who was a cynic! and the young ladies in the draper's shop shook their heads at each other and said, "Poor gentleman!" with the profoundest commiseration.

When he had left her, Polly threw out her skirts and smoothed the fur of her lovely new coat with a caressing hand. She felt that she loved it. It was more entirely delightful than even her husband—a happiness without alloy. She walked very slowly, enjoying every step of the way. She gave a penny to the beggar at the corner in the fulness of her satisfaction. So far her happiness had evidently a fine moral influence on Polly; and she was going to pay a visit, which was also very kind, to "the girls" in the River Lane. She was not one to forget old friends. She sailed along in her pride and glory through the quarter where she was so well known, and curved her nostrils at the smells, and allowed disgust to steal over her face when her path was crossed by an unlovely figure. Polly flattered herself that she was a fine lady complete; and there was no doubt that the imitation was very good in the general, so long as you did not enter into details.

At the entrance of the River Lane, however, she ceased to stand upon ceremony with herself. She picked up her skirts and went on at a more business-like rate of speed. Some one was coming up against the light, which by this time of the afternoon came chiefly from the west, someone with his shoulders up to his ears, who took off his hat to Polly, and pleased her until she perceived that it was only Law. "You here!" she said: and as she looked at him the moral influence of the sealskin almost vanished. Thus she went in state to visit the scenes in which so much of her previous life had passed. But a new sentiment was in Polly's eyes. She felt that she had a duty to do—a duty which was superior to benevolence. She pushed open the green swing door with a delicious sense of the difference. The girls were talking fast and loud when she opened the door, discussing some subject or other with all the natural chatter of the workroom. There was a pause when the sound of her heels and the rustle of her silk was heard—a hush ran round the table. How well Polly knew what it meant! "They will think it is a customer," she said to herself; and never customer swept in more majestically. They were all at work when she entered, as if they did not know what it was to chatter, and Ellen rose respectfully at the first appearance of the lady.

"Mother is upstairs, ma'am, but I can take any orders," she said; and then with a shriek cried out "Polly!"

"Polly!" echoed all the girls.

Here was a visitor indeed. They got up and made a circle round her, examining her and all she "had on." "In a sealskin!" 'Liza and Kate cried in a breath, with an admiration which amounted to awe. One of them even put forth her hand to stroke it in her enthusiasm. For an instant Polly allowed this fervour of admiration to have its way. Then she said, languidly—

"Give me a chair, please, and send Mrs. Welting to me. I wish to speak to Mrs. Welting. I am sorry to interrupt your work, young ladies—it is Mrs. Welting I want to see."

"But, Polly!" the girls cried all together. They were too much startled to know what to say. They stood gaping in a circle round her.

"I thought you had come to see us like a friend—like what you used to be."

"And weren't we all just glad to see you again, Polly—and quite the lady!" cried another. They would not take their dismissal at the first word.

"Young ladies," said Polly, "I've not come in any bad spirit. I don't deny as I've passed many a day here. My family (though always far above the dressmaking) was not well off, and I shall always be thankful to think as I did my best for them. But now that I'm married, in a different position," said Polly, "though always ready to stand your friend, when you want a friend, or to recommend you among the Abbey ladies, you can't think as I can go on with you like you were in my own sphere. Where there's no equality there can't be no friendship. Perhaps you wouldn't mind opening a window? It's rather early to put on my sealskin, but one never knows at this time of the year—and I'm 'eated with my walk. Send Mrs. Welting to me, please."

There was a great commotion among the girls. The two passive ones stood with open mouth, struck dumb by this magnificence.

"Lor!" cried Kate, finding no other word that could express her emotion.

Emma, though she was the youngest, was the most vehement of all. "I know what she's come for. She's come to make mischief," cried Emma. "I wouldn't fetch mother. I wouldn't go a step. Let her speak straight out what she's got to say."

"There's reason in everything," said Ellen. "You mayn't mean to keep us up like friends. Just as you like, I'm sure; none of us is wanting to keep it up; but mother takes no hand in the business, and that you know as well as me."

"Send Mrs. Welting to me," cried Polly, waving her hand majestically. She did not condescend to any further reply. She leant back on her chair and unfastened her beloved mantle at the throat. Then she 5 got out a laced handkerchief and fanned herself. "Me that thought it was so cold," Polly remarked to herself, "and it's like summer!" She did not pay any further attention to the young women, who consulted together with great indignation and excitement at a little distance.

"What can she have to say to mother? I wouldn't call mother, not if she was to sit there for a week," said Emma, who had a presentiment as to the subject of the visit.

"Lord! just look at her in her sealskin," interrupted Kate, who could think of nothing else.

But Ellen, who was the serious one, paused and hesitated. "We can't tell what it may be—and if it turned out to be a job, or something she had got us from some of the Abbey ladies! She's not bad natured," said Ellen, full of doubts.

All this time Polly waved her handkerchief about, with its edge of lace, fanning herself. She looked at no one—she was too much elevated above all the associations of the place to deign to take any notice. Had not she always been above it? With her disengaged hand she smoothed the fur of her sealskin, rubbing it knowingly upward. She was altogether unconscious of their talk and discussion. What could *they* have in common with Mrs. Despard? To see her, if any of her former associates had been cool enough to notice it, was still "as good as a play."

The upshot was, that while the others, with much ostentation of dragging their seats to the other end of the table, sat down and resumed their work with as much appearance of calm as possible, Ellen ran upstairs in obedience to her own more prudent suggestions, and reappeared shortly with her mother, a large, comely woman, who, not knowing who the visitor was, was a little expectant, hoping for a very good order—a trousseau, or perhaps mourning. "Or it might be the apartments," Mrs. Welting said. And when she entered the workroom she made the lady a curtsey, then cried out, as her daughters had done, "Why, bless my heart, Polly! The idea of taking me in like this, you saucy things," she cried, turning, laughing, upon the girls. But she did not get any response from these indignant young women, nor from Polly, who made no reply to her salutation, but sat still, delicately fanning herself.

Mrs. Welting stood between the two opposed parties, wondering what was the matter. Since Polly was here, she could have come only in friendship. "I'm sure I'm very glad to see you," she said, "and looking so well and so 'andsome. And what a lovely sealskin you've got on!"

"Mrs. Welting," said Polly, with great dignity, taking no notice of these friendly remarks, "I asked for you because I've something to say that is very particular. You don't take much charge of the business, but it is you as one must turn to about the girls. Mrs. Welting, you mayn't know, but there's goings on here as always gave me a deal of annoyance. And now I've come to tell you they must be put a stop to. I never could endure such goings on, and I mean to put a stop to them now."

"Lord bless us!" said Mrs. Welting. She was really alarmed. She gave a glance round upon her girls, all bursting with self-defence, and made them a sign to be silent. Then she turned to her visitor with a mixture of anxiety and defiance. "Speak up, Polly," she said; "nobody shall say as I won't listen, if there's anything against my girls; but speak up, for you've gone too far to stop now."

"How hot it is, to be sure!" said Mrs. Despard, "in this close bit of a place. I wish someone would open a window. I can't think how I could have put up with it so long. And I wonder what my 'usband would say if he heard me spoke to like that? I thought you would have the sense to understand that I've come here for your good. It wasn't to put myself on an equality with folks like you, working for your living. I don't want to be stuck up, but a lady must draw the line somewhere. Mrs. Welting, I don't suppose you know it—you ain't often in the workroom—it would be a deal better if you was. There's gentlemen comes here, till the place is known all over the town; and there is one young gentleman as I take a deal of interest in as makes me and his papa very uneasy all along of coming here—"

"Gentlemen! coming here!" cried Mrs. Welting, looking round upon her daughters with mingled anger and dismay.

"I know what I'm talking about," said Polly; "let them contradict me if they dare. He comes here mostly every day. One of the girls is that silly as to think he's after her. After her! I hope as he has more sense; he knows what's what a deal too well for that. He takes his fun out of them—that is what he does. But you may think yourself what kind of feelings his family has—the Captain and me. That's the one that encourages him most," Mrs. Despard added, pointing out Emma with her finger. "She is always enticing the poor boy to come here."

"Oh, you dreadful, false, wicked story!" cried Emma, flushed and crying. "Oh, mother, it ain't nothing of the kind! It was she as brought him first. She didn't mind who came when she was here. She said it was no harm, it was only a bit of fun. We was always against it—at least Ellen was," added the culprit, bursting forth into sobs and tears.

"Yes, I always was," said Ellen, demurely—it was not in human nature not to claim the palm of superior virtue—"but it was not Emma, it was Polly that began. I've heard her argue as it was no harm. She was the first with the Captain, and then when young Mr. Despard—"

"I am not going to sit here, and listen to abuse of my family," said Polly, rising. "I wouldn't have mentioned no names, for I can't abide to have one as belongs to me made a talk about in a place like this. I came to give you a warning, ma'am, not these hardened things. It isn't for nothing a lady in my position comes down to the River Lane. I've got my beautiful silk all in a muddle, and blacks upon a white bonnet is ruination. I did it for your sake, Mrs. Welting, for I've always had a respect for you. And now I've done my Christian duty," said Polly, with vehemence, shaking the dust from her blue silk. "There's them that talk about it, like that little Methody Ellen, but there ain't many that do it. But don't let anybody suppose," she cried, growing hotter and hotter, "that I mean to do it any more! If you let him come here after this, I won't show you any mercy—we'll have the law of you, my 'usband and I. There's laws against artful girls as entice poor innocent young men. Don't you go for to think," cried Mrs. Despard, sweeping out while they all gazed after her, speechless, "because I've once done my Christian duty that I'm going to do it any more!"

We will not attempt to describe the commotion that followed—the reproaches, the tears, the fury of the girls betrayed, of which none was more hot than that of Ellen, who had to stand and hear herself called a Methody—she who was conscious of being an Anglican and a Catholic without blemish, and capable of anything in the world before Dissent.

Polly sailed up the hill, triumphant in that consciousness of having done her duty as a Christian, but equally determined not to do it any more; and what with the consciousness of this noble performance, and what with the sealskin, found it in her power to be almost agreeable to her step-daughter, when the Captain, who, after all, was Lottie's father, and did not like the idea that his girl should be banished from his house, had met her and brought her in.

"She has not had the careful bringing-up that you have had, my child," the Captain said. "She hasn't had your advantages. You must have a little patience with her, for my sake." Captain Despard had always been irresistible when he asked tenderly, with his head on one side, and an insinuating roll in his voice, that anything should be done for his sake.

Lottie, who was happy in the sense of her lover's readiness to sacrifice everything for her sake (as she thought), and to whom the whole world seemed fairer in consequence, yielded without any struggle; while Polly, on her part, put on her most gracious looks.

"If you take every word I say for serious," said Polly, "I don't know whatever I shall do. I never was used to have my words took up hasty like that. I say a deal of naughtiness that I don't mean—don't I, Harry? You and me would never have come together, should we, if you'd always gone and taken me at my word?" And so the reconciliation was effected, and things went on as before. There was no similar occurrence in respect to Law, whose looks at Polly were murderous; but, then, Law had no delicacy of sentiment, and, whatever had happened, would have come into his meals all the same.

CHAPTER XXXVI
FAMILY DUTY: BY A FINER ARTIST

Rollo did not come away from the strange excitement of that interview on the Slopes with the same feelings which filled the mind of Lottie. The first intense sensation of shame with which he had realised the villany of the proposal which Lottie did not understand soon changed into a different sentiment. He had felt its guilt, its treacherous cruelty, under the guise of devotion, far more bitterly and intensely than as if she had understood and denounced him; and the relief of his escape from an indignation and horror which must have been as overwhelming as the confidence, had made him feel how great a danger he had run, and how terrible to him, as well as to her, would have been the discovery of his base intention. How could he ever think that Lottie, proud, and pure, and fearless of evil as she was, could have fallen into such a snare! He felt himself a fool as well as a villain; perceiving, too, by the light of fact, what he would not have understood in theory, that the very uncomprehension of innocence makes guilt contemptible as well as terrible. If she could have understood him, he would scarcely have felt so mean, so miserable, so poor a creature as he did now; not even a gay and fine betrayer, but a pitiful cheat and would-be criminal, false to everything that nature trusts in. Rollo had not been irreproachable hitherto; but such sins as he had indulged in had been done among those who were sinners like himself, among people who had a cynical comprehension of the worth of promises and the value of vows. He had never tried that *rôle* of the seducer before; and the fact that his own shame and horror were real made them all the more hard to bear. Shame, however, of this bitter kind is not an improving influence. Soon it began to turn to anger equally bitter. He tried to think that Lottie was partly to blame, that she had "led him on," that he never would have gone so far but for "encouragement" from her. Even it flashed across his mind that she was not so unconscious as she appeared, but had pretended ignorance in order to rivet her chains upon him, and force him to the more honourable way which was so much more for her interest. He tried to force this idea into his own mind, which was not sufficiently depraved to receive it; but yet it was not long before he was angry, irritated against the girl who would not understand him, and sore with the humiliation she had inflicted unawares.

Other influences, too, came in to break the purer spell of honourable love under which Rollo, to his own surprise, had so entirely fallen. With the return of Augusta and her husband, the world seemed to have come back and seized him. Even the society of Augusta, of itself, had an immediate influence, breaking up the magic of the seclusion in which he had been content to live. Lady Caroline was not a woman who could be called unworldly, but she was passive, and did not take any initiative even in the way of gossip. She liked to hear it; there came a little gleam of interest to her eyes when the stories of the great world were brought to her, when she was told who was going to marry who, and by what schemes and artifices the marriage had been brought about; and who had most frequently and boldly broken the marriage vow, and by whom it had been most politely eluded; and how everybody lived and cheated, and nothing was as it seemed; and all that is done for money, and that is done for pleasure, in that busy, small, narrow-minded village society—which is the world. But though she loved to hear, she could not begin; for, unless people told her what was going on, how, she sometimes asked piteously, was she to know? As for the Dean, he was not in the habit of it any more than his wife, though when he went to town he would bring down invariably a piece of news from his club—of somebody's appointment, or somebody's good luck, or somebody's wedding. "Now, why can't you go and do likewise?" he would say to Rollo. But all this was mild and secondary in comparison with Augusta, who brought the very air of what Mr. Jenkins calls the Upper Ten into the Deanery, perfuming all the rooms and all the meals with stories of fortunes won and lost, of squabbles, ministerial and domestic, of marriages and dinners alike "arranged," and all the wonderful *dessous des cartes* and *behind the scenes* with which so many people are acquainted in fashionable life. Who so well as Augusta knew that when the Duke of Mannering gave up his governorship, it was not from any political reason, but because the life he led was such that the place was far too hot to hold him, and Government was only too glad to send out Algy Fairfax, though he was only a younger son, and had no particular interest, simply to smooth things down? And what a lucky thing it was for Algy to be there just at the right moment, when there was nobody else handy, and just when Lord Arthur was there, who had got him to explain matters to his elder brother, and knew what he could do! It was what old Lady Fairfax had been scheming for all her life, just as she had been scheming to catch young Snellgrove for Mina. Of course she had succeeded. Mina was almost distracted, everybody knew. It was she who had that affair with Lord Colbrookdale, and now everybody said she was wildly in love with Reginald Fane, her cousin; but she might just as well be in love with St. Paul's, for he had not a penny, and she was to be married directly. Did you hear about her settlements? They were simply ridiculous. But that old woman was wonderful. There was nothing she did not think of, and everything she wanted she got. And then there was that story about poor young Jonquil, of the War Department, who married somebody quite out of the question, a poor clergyman's daughter, or something of that sort, without a penny (though he might have had the rich Miss Windsor Brown for the asking, people said), and of the dreadful end he had come to, living down in some horrid weedy little cottage about Kew, and wheeling out two babies in a perambulator. All these tales, and a thousand more, Augusta told, filling the Deanery with a shameful train of people, all doing something they did not want to do, or forcing others to do it, or following their pleasure through every law, human and divine. Lady Caroline sat in her easy-chair (she was not allowed to put up her feet except in the evening, after dinner, when Augusta was at home), and listened with half-closed eyes, but unfailing attention. "I knew his father very well," she would say now and then, or "his mother was a great friend of mine." As for Rollo, he knew all the people of whom these stories were told. He had seen the things beginning of which his cousin knew all the conclusions, and what went on behind the scenes, and thus he was carried back after the idyll of the last six weeks to his own proper world. He began to feel that there was no world but that, that nothing else could make up for the want of it; and a shudder ran over him when he thought of Jonquil's fate. Augusta, for her part, did not conceal her surprise to find him at the Deanery. "What is Rollo doing here?" she said to her mother.

"I am sure, my dear, I do not know. He seems to like it, and we are very glad to have him," Lady Caroline replied. But that did not satisfy Mrs. Daventry's curiosity. What could a young man of fashion, a man of the world, do here?

"I wonder what he is after," she said; "I wonder what his object can be. It can't be only your society and papa's. I should just like to know what he is up to. He is not a fool, to have gone and got entangled somehow. I wonder what he can mean by it!" Augusta cried; but her mother could give her no idea. Lady Caroline thought it was natural enough.

"I don't see that it is so strange," she said. "Autumn is a terrible time. To sleep in a strange bed night after night, and never settle down anywhere! Rollo likes to be comfortable; and then there is this Miss Despard. You have heard about Miss Despard?"

"What about Miss Despard?" Augusta said, pricking up her ears.

"She is to be the prima donna," said Lady Caroline. "He thinks she will make his fortune. He has always got some wild scheme in his head. He used to annoy me very much to have her here—"

"And did you have her here?" cried Augusta, roused into sudden excitement. "Oh, why didn't I know of it! I thought there must be some reason! Lottie Despard! And were you obliged to have her here, mamma? What a bore it must have been for you!"

"I did not like it, my dear," her ladyship said. But after a while she added, conscience compelling her, "She sang very nicely, Augusta; she has a pretty voice."

"She has plenty of voice, but she cannot sing a note," said Augusta, with vehemence, who was herself, without any voice to speak of, a very well-trained musician. She would not say any more to frighten Lady Caroline, but she took her measures without delay. And the result of Augusta's enquires was that Rollo found his feet entangled in a web of engagements which separated him from Lottie. But though he was sore and angry, he had not given up Lottie, nor had he any intention so to do. When, however, the day came for Lottie's next lesson, Mrs. Daventry herself did the Signor the honour of calling upon him just before his pupil appeared. "You know the interest I always took in Lottie. Please let me stay. We have so many musical friends in town that I am sure I can be of use to her," Mrs. Daventry said; and the consequence was that when Lottie and her companion entered the Signor's sitting-room, the great chair between the fire and the window in which Mrs. O'Shaughnessy usually placed herself was found to be already occupied by the much greater lady, whose sudden appearance in this cordial little company put everybody out. Augusta sat leaning back in the big chair, holding a screen between her cheek and the fire, her fine Paris bonnet, her furs, and her velvet making a great appearance against the dark wall, and her smiles and courtesy confounding every individual of the familiar party. She was more refined, far less objectionable than Polly, and did her spiriting in a very different way; but there could be little doubt that the fine artist was also the most effectual. She put the entire party out, from the least to the greatest, though the sweetest of smiles was on her face. Even the Signor was not himself with this gracious personage superintending his exertions. He was a good English Tory, of the most orthodox sentiments; but he was at the same time an impatient Italian, of despotic tastes, and did not easily tolerate the position of second in his own house. Rollo, who had determined to be present, whatever happened, but who, by a refinement of cruelty, did not know his cousin was coming, came in with all the ease of habit, and had already betrayed the fact of his constant attendance at these strange lessons, when Augusta called to him, covering him with confusion. "We shall be quite a family party," she said. "I'm so glad you take an interest in poor Lottie *too*." Rollo could not but ask himself what was the meaning of this sudden friendliness and interest; but he was obliged to place himself by her side when she called him. And when Lottie came in, at whom he did not dare to look, his position became very uncomfortable. Mrs. O'Shaughnessy, finding her seat occupied, and herself compelled to take a lower place, sat down on a chair near the door, with wrath which made her countenance flame. She had stood up in the room a minute before she seated herself, looking round for a more comfortable place, and had greeted Mr. Ridsdale joyously as an old friend. But even Rollo, usually so polite, who never saw her without doing his very best to make himself agreeable, even he never attempted to introduce her to his cousin, and the good woman sat down accordingly, against the wall, silent and fuming, while Augusta took the chief place. The stranger in the midst of them turned the whole party upside down. Even Purcell was so occupied by the conversation that was kept up in whispers by Augusta, in her corner, even during the singing, that he missed to turn the leaves at the proper moment. Augusta knew very well what she was doing. She had a respect for the Signor, but she had higher purposes in hand. She kept Rollo by her side, and kept up a conversation with him through all, which was, like her usual conversation, deeply pervaded by the essence of society and "the Upper Ten." She kept it up in a whisper when Lottie began to sing. "Don't you think she is handsome? She is a little like Lady Augustus Donjon about the eyes—don't you think so? Oh, I never told you that good story about the Augustus Donjons," said Mrs. Daventry; and she told her story, all through the song, half audible.

"Wasn't it good?" Augusta said; and then, "That is such a pretty song; and, Lottie, you are so improved, I should never have known it to be the same voice. Yes, wasn't it good, Rollo? Augustus Donjon is always the first to laugh himself, and even the children have got it in the nursery. She is such a jolly woman, she never minds. What are we going to have next? Oh, that will be very nice!" said Augusta.

Was it wonderful that Purcell should lose the place? The young fellow did all he could to stop the fine lady with furious glances; and the Signor, though his back was turned to her, felt the whisper and the indignity run through every nerve of him. Even in his back you could see, Purcell thought, how horribly annoyed he was. His sensitive shoulders winced and shuddered, his elbows jerked. He could not attend to his accompaniment, he could not attend to his pupil. In the very midst of a song he said aloud, distracted by the s's of a whisper which was louder than usual, "This must never happen again." As for Lottie, she did not know what she was doing. She sang—because it was the hour for her lesson, because she found herself standing there by the side of the Signor's piano—but not for any other reason. She had neither inspiration, nor had she that nascent sense that Art might perhaps console for other losses which she had once felt when Rollo was away. She was distracted by the whispering behind her, from which she could not withdraw her attention. Why did he listen? Why did he allow Augusta to draw him into unfaithfulness to her? And yet, how could he help it? Was it not all Augusta's fault? But with whomsoever the fault lay, Lottie was the victim. Her voice could not be got out. And the reader knows that Augusta was right—that this poor girl, though she had the voice of an angel, did not as yet know how to sing, and had no science to neutralise the impressions made upon her which took away all her heart and her voice. She went on making a brave fight; but when once the Signor faltered in his accompaniment, and said loud out, "This must never happen again," and when Purcell forgot to turn the page, what is it to be supposed Lottie could do, who was not the tenth part of a musician such as they were? She faltered, she went wrong. Tune she could not help keeping, it was in her nature: even her wrong notes were never out of harmony; but in time she went wildly floundering, not even kept right by the Signor. Even that did not matter very much, seeing that none of these people, who generally were so critical, so censorious, so ready to be hard upon her out of pure anxiety for her, were in a state of mind to perceive the mistakes she was making. And it was only vaguely that Lottie herself was aware of them. Her whole attention was attracted in spite of herself by the whispering in the corner.

"Oh, thank you so much!" Augusta broke forth, when she came to the end. "What a charming bit that is! It is Schubert, of course, but I don't know it. The time was a little odd, but the melody was beautiful."

"You know my weakness," said the Signor stiffly, turning round. "I cannot answer for myself when people are talking. I am capable of doing anything that is wrong."

"Oh! I remember," cried Mrs. Daventry; "you used to be very stern with all our little societies. Not a word were we allowed to say. We all thought it hard, but of course it was better for us in the long run. And are you as tyrannical as ever, Signor?"

"Not so tyrannical since ladies come here, and carry on their charming conversation all the same. I only wish I could have profited by it. It seemed amusing and instructive. If I were not unhappily one of those poor creatures who can only do one thing at a time—"

"Oh, Signor, how very severe you are!" said Augusta. "I was only telling my cousin some old stories which I am sure you must have heard weeks ago. You know the Donjons? No! Oh, I thought everybody knew the Augustus Donjons! They go everywhere; they have friends in music and friends in art, and you meet all sorts of people at their house. Lottie, when you are a great singer, I hope you will remember me, and send me cards now and then for one of your concerts. There are so many things going on now, and all so expensive, that people in our circumstances really can't do everything. Spencer has stalls where we go when there is anything particular; but I assure you, now-a-days, one can no more afford a box at the opera—! You know, Signor; but I daresay your friends always find you places somewhere."

"That is true. If everything else fails, a friend of mine who plays second violin will lend me his instrument," said the Signor, "or a box-keeper now and then will be glad of an evening's holiday. They are *blasés*, these people. They do not care if Patti sings. They will rather have a holiday and go to a music-hall."

Augusta looked at her cousin, puzzled. She did not see the irony. After all, she thought, there was not, perhaps, so very much difference between a musician and those perfectly gentlemanlike people who showed you to your box or your stall. She had often thought how nice they looked. The Signor saw her bewilderment, and added, with a smile—"You have never recognised me in my borrowed part?"

"Oh, Signor!—certainly not. I never meant to say anything that would suggest—to imply anything that might—indeed, I hope you will not think I have been indiscreet," cried Augusta. "But, Rollo, we must go, we must certainly go. I told mamma you would come with me to see the old Skeffingtons. Spencer is away, and I must return their call. Signor, I do hope you will forgive me. I meant nothing that was disagreeable. I am sure we are all put to worse straits than that, in order to get a little amusement without ruining ourselves. Oh, Rollo, *please* come away!"

Rollo had snatched an instant as Lottie gathered her music together. "It is not my fault," he said. "She never lets me alone. I did not know she was coming here to-day. Do not put on that strange look."

"Have I a strange look?" Lottie said. What ups and downs were hers!—the other day so triumphant, and now again so cast down and discouraged. The tears were standing in her eyes, but she looked at him bravely. "It does not matter," she said; "perhaps she does not mean it. It takes away my heart, and then I have not any voice."

"Oh, my love!" he whispered under his breath. "And I must put up with it all. At the elm-tree, dear, to-night."

"Oh, no, no!" she said.

"Why no no? it is not my fault. Dear, for pity—"

"What are you saying to Miss Despard, Rollo? I am jealous of you, Lottie; my cousin never comes to my lessons. And, indeed, I wonder the Signor allows it. It is very delightful for us, but how you can work, really *work* with such a train!" Augusta turned round and looked severely at Mrs. O'Shaughnessy. "If I were the Signor I should not admit one creature except your maid."

But this was an indignity which mortal could not endure. The kind Irishwoman rose to her feet as quickly as the low chair would permit. "And sure, I agree with the lady," she said. "Lottie, me love, I can bear a deal for you, and I've stood your friend through thick and thin, as all here knows. But come again to the Signor's I won't, not if you were to go down on your knees—unless he gives his word of honour that them that hasn't a scrap of manners, them that don't know how to behave themselves, that whispers when you're singing, and interrupts when you're speaking, will never be here again to insult you—at least not when Mistress O'Shaughnessy's here."

Leaving this fine outburst of indignation to vibrate through the room, Mrs. O'Shaughnessy turned upon her heel, and, grasping Lottie by the arm, took the *pas* from Augusta, and marched out with blazing eyes and countenance flushed with war. "Ye can bring the music," she said to old Pick, who had been listening, and whose disappointment at Lottie's break-down was great, "and there'll be a shilling for you. I'd scorn to be beholden to one of them." Rollo made an anxious attempt, but in vain, to catch Lottie's eyes as she was swept past him. But Lottie would not return his glance. Augusta had done a great deal more execution with her subtle tactics than Polly with hers—which, perhaps, were not more brutal because they were so much less refined.

"What an odious woman!" Augusta cried; "walking out of the room before *me*. But, Rollo, she was quite right, though she was so impudent. You ought not to go there. Mamma says you want Lottie Despard for your new opera. She would never do. She has a voice, but she doesn't know how to sing. A good audience would never put up with her."

"That is all a mistake," said Rollo; "it may be very well to know how to sing, but it is much better to have a voice."

"I could not have supposed you were so old-fashioned; never say that in public if you want anyone to have any opinion of you. But even if you are so sure of her you should keep away; you should not interfere with her training. The fact is," said Augusta, very seriously, "I am dreadfully afraid you have got into some entanglement even now."

"You are very kind," said Rollo, smiling, "to take such care of me."

"I wish I could take a great deal more care. I am almost sure you have got into some entanglement, though, of course, you will say no. But, Rollo, you know, you might as well hang yourself at once. You could never hold up your head again. I don't know what on earth would become of you. Uncle Courtland would wash his hands of you, and what could any of your friends do? It would be moral suicide," said Augusta, with solemnity. "I told you about young Jonquil, and the state he was in. Rollo! that's the most miserable thing that can happen to a man; other things may go wrong, and mend again; your people may interpose, or a hundred things may happen; but this sort of thing is without hope. Oh, Rollo, take it to heart! There are many things a man may do that don't tell half so much against him. You would be poor, and everybody would give you up. For goodness' sake, Rollo, think of what I say."

He gave her an answer which was not civil; and, as he went along by her side to old Canon Skeffington's, there suddenly gleamed across his mind a recollection of the elm-tree on the Slopes, and all the sweetness of the stolen hours which had passed there. And Lottie had said "No." Why should she have said "No?" It seemed to him that he cared for nothing else so much as to know why for this first time she had refused to meet him. Had she began to understand his proposition? had she found out what it was he meant? Was she afraid of him, or indignant, or—? But she had not looked indignant. Of all things in the world, there was nothing he wanted so much as to know what Lottie meant by that refusal. Yet, notwithstanding, he did take to heart what Augusta said.

CHAPTER XXXVII
ANOTHER CHANCE

Mr. Ashford, the Minor Canon, had, anyone would have supposed, as tranquil yet as pleasantly occupied a life as a man could have. He had not very much of a clergyman's work to do. There was no need for him to harass himself about the poor, who are generally a burden upon the shoulders or hung about the neck of the parish priest; he was free from that weight which he had found himself unable to bear. He had only the morning and evening prayers to think of, very rarely even a sermon. Most clergymen like that part of their duties; they like to have it in their power to instruct, to edify, or even to torture the community in general, with perfect safety from any reprisals; but Ernest Ashford in that, as in many other things, was an exception to the general rule in his profession. He was not fond of sermons, and consequently it was a very happy thing for him that so few were required of him. He was now and then tormented by his pupils, which brought his life within the ordinary conditions of humanity; otherwise, with his daily duty in the beautiful Abbey, which was a delight to him, and the leisure of his afternoons and evenings, and the landscape that lay under his window, and the antique grace of his little house, and all his books, no existence could have been more unruffled and happy. He was as far lifted above those painful problems of common life which he could not solve, and which had weighed upon him like personal burdens in the beginning of his career, as his window was above the lovely sweep of country at the foot of the hill. What had he to do but sing Handel, to read and to muse, and to be content? These were the natural conditions of his life.

But it would appear that these conditions are not fit for perverse humanity; for few indeed are the persons so happily exempt from ordinary troubles who do not take advantage of every opportunity to drag themselves into the arena and struggle like their neighbours. Mrs. Ashford did this in what may be called the most wanton and unprovoked way. What business had he to take any interest in Lottie Despard? She was out of his sphere; the Abbey stood between them, a substantial obstacle; and many things a great deal more important—social differences, circumstances that tended to separate rather than to bring together. And it was not even in the orthodox and regular way that he had permitted this girl to trouble his life. He might have fallen in love with her, seeing her so often in the Abbey (for Lottie's looks were remarkable enough to attract any man), and nobody could have found fault. It is true, a great many people would have found fault, in all likelihood people who had nothing to do with it and no right to interfere, but who would, as a matter of course, have pitied the poor man who had been beguiled, and indignantly denounced the designing girl; but no one would have had any right to interfere. As a clergyman of the Church of England Mr. Ashford had absolute freedom to fall in love if he pleased, and to marry if he pleased, and nobody would have dared to say a word. But he had not done this: he had not fallen in love, and he did not think of marriage; but being himself too tranquil in his well-being, without family cares or anxieties, perhaps out of the very forlornness of his happiness, his attention had been fixed—was it upon the first person he had encountered in the midst of a moral struggle harder, and therefore nobler, than his own quiescent state? Perhaps this was all. He could never be sure whether it was the girl fighting to keep her father and brother out of the mire, fighting with them to make them as honest and brave herself, or whether it was simply Lottie that interested him. Possibly it was better not to enter into this question. She was the most interesting person within his range. His brethren the Canons, Minor and Major, were respectable or dignified clergymen, very much like the rest of the profession. Within the Abbey precincts there was nobody with any particular claim upon the sympathy of his fellows, or whose moral position demanded special interest. The Uxbridges were anxious about their son, who was a careless boy, not any better than Law; but then the father and mother were quite enough to support that anxiety, and kept it to themselves as much as possible. It was not a matter of life and death, as in Law's case, who had neither father nor mother to care what became of him, but only Lottie—a creature who herself ought to have been cared for and removed far from all such anxieties. Even the deficiency in Lottie's character—the pain with which she was brought to see that she must herself adopt the profession which was within her reach, and come out from the shelter of home and the menial work with which she was contented, to earn money and make an independence for herself—had given her a warmer hold upon the spectator, who, finding himself unable to struggle against the world and himself, had withdrawn from that combat, yet never could quite pardon himself for having withdrawn. She, poor child, could not withdraw; she was compelled to confront the thing she hated by sheer force of necessity, and had done so—compelled, indeed, but only as those who can are compelled. Would she have fled from the contemplation of want and pain as he had done? Would she have allowed herself incapable to bear the consequences of the duty set before her, whatever it might be? Sometimes Mr. Ashford would ask himself this question: though what could be more ridiculous than the idea that a girl of twenty could judge better than a man of five-and-thirty? But he was interested in her by very reason of her possession of qualities which he did not possess. He had given her good advice, and she had taken it; but even while he gave it and pressed it upon her he had been thinking what would she have said to his problems, how would she have decided for him? All this increased his interest in Lottie. He realised, almost more strongly than she did herself, all the new difficulties that surrounded her; he divined her love, which pained him not less than the other troublous circumstances in her lot, since he could not imagine it possible that any good could come out of such a connection. That Rollo Ridsdale would marry anyone but an heiress his superior knowledge of the world forced him to doubt; he could not believe in a real honest love, ending in a marriage, between the Chevalier's daughter and Lady Caroline's nephew. And accordingly this, which seemed to Lottie to turn her doubtful future into a certainty of happiness, seemed to Mr. Ashford the worst of all the dangers in her lot. It would be no amusement for her, as it would be for the other; and what was to become of the girl with her father's wife in possession of her home and such a lover in possession of her heart? His spectatorship got almost more than he could bear at times; nobody seemed to see as he did, and he was the last person in the world who could interfere to save her. Could anyone save her? He could not tell; he knew no one who would take the office upon himself; but least of all could he do it. He watched with interest which had grown into the profoundest anxiety—an anxiety which in its turn was increased tenfold by the sense that there was nothing which he could do.

Such were the feelings in his mind when the Signor joined him on his homeward way after service on the afternoon when Mrs. Daventry had so interrupted Lottie's lesson. Augusta had sailed up the aisle and out by the door in the cloisters which adjoined the Deanery, as they came out of the room where all the surplices were hanging in their old presses, and where the clergy robed themselves. The two men came out when the rustle and flutter of the party of ladies were still in the air, and old Wykeham looking after them with cynical criticism. The hassocks in the aisles, which had been placed there for the convenience of the overflowing congregations, too great for the Abbey choir, which crowded every corner now and then, were all driven about like boats at sea by the passage of these billows of trailing silk, and Wykeham had stooped to put them back into their places. Stooping did not suit the old man, and he could not do without his natural growl. "I wish they'd stick to 'em," he said; "plenty of dirt sticks to 'em. They sweeps up the aisles and saves us trouble; but I'd just like one o' them heavy hassocks to stick."

"And so should I," said the Signor under his breath. "They are insufferable," he said with vehemence as he emerged into the cloister. "I have made up my mind I shall not allow any intrusion again."

"Who are insufferable, and what is the intrusion you are going to prevent?" said the Minor Canon with a smile.

"Ashford," said the Signor with much heat, "I am not going to have you come any more to Miss Despard's lessons. Don't say anything to me on the subject; I know all about interest and so forth, but I can't permit it. It's ruin to her, and it irritates me beyond bearing. Interest? if you take any real interest in her you would see that nothing could be less for her welfare, nothing more destructive of any chances she may have—"

"My dear Rossinetti, I never was present at Miss Despard's lesson but once."

"It was once too much, then," the Signor cried. "The girl is getting ruined. That woman, that Mrs. Daventry—you should have heard her whispering behind our backs with her fan in front of her face, then stopping a moment to say, 'What a pretty song: how much you have improved.'"

The Signor made an attempt to mimic Augusta, but he had no talent that way, and the mincing tone to which he gave utterance was like nothing that had ever been heard before. But if his imitation was bad his disgust was quite genuine. He could not think of anything else; he returned again and again to the subject as they went on.

"The upper classes," he said, "are famous for good manners. This is their good manners: Two of them thrust themselves in for their amusement to a place where a poor girl is working hard at art, and a man who has spent most of his life in learning is trying to transmit his knowledge to her. And the moment that girl begins singing *they* begin their loathsome chatter about Mr. this and My Lady that. Do not say anything to me, Ashford; I tell you, you shall not come, you nor anyone else, again."

"Is she making progress?" said the Minor Canon.

"Progress? how could she, with that going on? No; sometimes she will sing like an angel, sometimes like—anyone. It drives me wild! And then our gracious patrons appear—Mr. Ridsdale (who ought to know better) and Mrs. Daventry. I ought to know better too; I will defend my doors from henceforth. To be sure, I did not mean that; *you* may come if you like."

"And Mr. Ridsdale talked? How did she bear it?" said Mr. Ashford nervously.

"It is I who will not bear it," said the musician. "And these are people who pretend to love music—pretend to know: it is insufferable. If she ever becomes a great singer—"

"If? I thought you had no doubt."

"How was I to know I should be intruded upon like this? Poor girl. I think, after all, the best thing for her will be to marry my boy, John Purcell, and live a quiet life."

"Marry—Purcell?"

"Why not? He is a very good musician; he will live to make a great deal of money: he has genius—positively genius. The best thing she could do would be to marry him. She is too sensitive. Susceptibility belongs to the artist temperament, but then it must be susceptibility within control. Her voice flutters like a flame when the wind is blowing. Sometimes it blows out altogether. And he loves her. She will do best to marry my John."

"You cannot have so little perception, Rossinetti. How can you entertain such an idea for a moment? Purcell?"

"In what is he so inferior?" said the Signor with quiet gravity. "He is young, not like you and me. That is a great deal. He is an excellent musician, and he has a home to offer to her. I should advise it if she would take my advice. It would not harm her in her career to marry a musician, if finally she accepts her career. She has not accepted it yet," said the Signor with a sigh.

"Then all your certainty is coming to nothing," said Mr. Ashford, "and Ridsdale's—"

"Ah, Ridsdale—that is what harms her. Something might be done if he were out of the way. He is an influence that is too much for me. Either she has heard of his new opera, and expects to have her place secured in it, under his patronage, or else she hopes—something else." The Signor kept his eyes fixed upon his companion. He wanted to surprise Mr. Ashford's opinion without giving his own.

"Do you think," said the Minor Canon indignantly, "even with the little you know of her, that she is a girl to calculate upon having a place secured to her, or upon anyone's patronage?"

"Then she hopes for—something else; which is a great deal worse for her happiness," said the Signor. Then there was a pause. They had reached Mr. Ashford's door, but he did not ask his companion to go in. The Signor paused, but he had not ended what he had to say: "With the little I know of her"—he said—"do you know more?"

This was not an easy question to answer. He could not say, I have been watching her for weeks; I know almost all that can be found out; but, serious man as he was, Mr. Ashford was embarrassed. He cleared his throat, and indeed even went through a fit of coughing to gain time. "Her brother is my pupil," he said at last, "and, unfortunately, he likes better to talk than to work. I have heard a great deal about her. I think I know enough to say that she would not hope—anything that she had not been wooed and persuaded to believe in—"

"Then you think—you really suppose—you are so credulous, so optimist, so romantic," cried the Signor with a *crescendo* of tone and gesticulation—"you think that a man of the world, a man of society, with no money, would marry—for love?"

The musician broke into a short laugh. "You should have heard them," he added after a dramatic pause, "this very day whispering, chuchotéing, in my room while she was singing—talking—oh, don't you know what about? About girls who marry rich men while (they say) their hearts are breaking for poor ones—about women using the most shameless arts to entrap a rich man, and even playing devotion to a woman with money; and the only one to be really pitied of all is the poor fellow, who has followed his heart, who is poor, who lives at Kew, and has two babies in a perambulator. I laugh at him myself," said the Signor—"the fool, to give up his club and society because he took it into his silly head to love!"

"Rossinetti," said the Minor Canon, "I know there are quantities of these wretched stories about; but human nature is human nature, after all, not the pitiful thing they make it out. I don't believe they are true."

"What! after all the newspapers—the new branch of literature that has sprung from them?" cried the Signor. Then he paused again and subsided. "I am of your opinion," he said. "The fire would come down from heaven if it was true; but *they* believe it: that is the curious thing. You and I, we are not in society; we are charitable; we say human nature never was so bad as that; but they believe it. Rollo Ridsdale would be ashamed to behave like a man, as you and I would feel ourselves forced to behave, as my boy John is burning to do."

"You and I." The Minor Canon scarcely knew how it was that he repeated these words; they caught his ear and dropped from his lips before he was aware.

The Signor looked at him with a smile which was half satire and a little bit sympathy. He said, "That is what you are coming to, Ashford. I see it in your eye."

"You are speaking—folly," said Mr. Ashford; then he added hastily, "I have got one of my boys coming. I must go in."

"Good-day," said the other with his dark smile. He had penetrated the secret thoughts that had not as yet taken any definite form in his friend's breast. Sometimes another eye sees more clearly than our own what is coming uppermost in our minds—or at least its owner believes so. The Signor was all the more likely to be right in this, that he had no belief in the calm sentiment of "interest" as actuating a man not yet too old for warmer feelings, in respect to a woman. He smiled sardonically at Platonic affection—as most people indeed do, unless the case is their own. He knew but one natural conclusion in such circumstances, and settled that it would be so without more ado. And such reasoning is sure in the majority of cases to be right, or to help to make itself right by the mere suggestion. To be sure he took an "interest"—a great interest—in Lottie himself; but that was in the way of art.

Mr. Ashford had no boy coming that he knew of when he said this to escape from the Signor; but, as sometimes happens, the expedient justified itself, and he had scarcely seated himself in his study when some one came up the oak staircase two or three steps at a time, and knocked at his door. In answer to the "Come in," which was said with some impatience—for the Minor Canon had a great deal to think about, and had just decided to subject himself to a cross-examination—who should open the door but Law—Law, without any book under his arm, and with a countenance much more awake and alive than on the occasions when he carried that sign of study. "Can I speak to you?" Law said, casting a glance round the room to see that no one else was there. He came in half suspicious, but with serious meaning on his face. Then he came and placed himself in the chair which stood between Mr. Ashford's writing-table and his bookcases. "I want to ask your advice," he said.

"Well; I have done nothing else but give you my advice for some time past, Law."

"Yes—to work—I know. You have given me a great deal of that sort of advice. What good is it, Mr. Ashford? I've gone on week after week, and what will it ever come to? Well, I know what you are going to say. I work, but I don't work. I don't care a bit about it. I haven't got my heart in it. It is quite true. But you can't change your disposition; you can't change your nature."

"Stop a little, Law. So far as work is concerned you often can, if you will—"

"Ah, but there's the rub," said Law, looking his Mentor in the face. "I don't want to—that is the simple fact. I don't feel that I've the least desire to. I feel as if I won't even when I know I ought. I think it's more honest now at last to tell you the real truth."

"I think I knew it pretty well some time ago," said the Minor Canon with a smile. "It is a very common complaint. Even that can be got over with an effort. Indeed, I am glad you have found it out. Perhaps even, you know, it is not your brain at all but your will that is at fault."

"Mr. Ashford," said Law solemnly, "what is the good of talking? You know and I know that I never could make anything of it if I were to work, as we call it, till I was fifty. I never could pass any examination. They would be fools indeed if they let me in. I am no real good for anything like that. You know it well enough; why shouldn't you say it? Here are you and me alone—nobody to overhear us, nobody to be vexed. What is the use of going on in the old way? I shall never do any good. You know it just as well as I."

"Law," said Mr. Ashford, "I will not contradict you. I believe you are right. If there was any other way of making your living I should say you were right. Books are not your natural tools; but they open the door to everything. The forest service, the telegraph service—all that sort of thing would suit you."

At this point Law got up with excitement, and began walking up and down the room. "That is all very well," he said. "Mr. Ashford, what is the use of deceiving ourselves? I shall never get into any of these. I've come to ask your advice once for all. I give up the books; I could only waste more time, and I've wasted too much already. It has come to this: I'll emigrate or I'll 'list. I don't see how I'm to do that even, for I've no money—not enough to take me to London, let alone Australia. Why shouldn't I do the other? It's good enough; if there was a war it would be good enough. Even garrison duty I shouldn't mind. It wouldn't hurt *my* pride," the lad said with a sudden flush of colour that belied his words; "and I might go away from here, so that it would not hurt *her*. That's all, Mr. Ashford," he said with suppressed feeling. "Only her—she's the only one that cares; and if I went away from here she would never know."

"Has anything happened to drive you to a decision at once? Is there anything new—anything—?"

"There is always something new," said Law. "That woman has been to—to the only place I ever cared to go—to shut the door against me. They were her own friends too—at least people as good as—a great deal better than she. She has been there to bully them on my account, to say they are not to have me. Do you think I'll stand that? What has she to do with me?"

"It must be a great deal worse for your sister, Law."

"Well, isn't that what I say? Do you think I can stand by and see Lottie bullied? Once she drove her out of the house. By Jove, if Lottie hadn't come home I'd have killed her. I shouldn't have stopped to think; I should have killed her," said Law, whose own wrong had made him desperate. "Do you think I can stand by and see Lottie bullied by that woman? She's brought it partly upon herself. She was too hard in the house with her management both upon the governor and me. She meant it well, but she was too hard.

But still she's Lottie, and I can't see her put upon. Do you think I am made of stone," cried Law indignantly, "or something worse than stone?"

"But if you were in Australia what better would she be? There you would certainly be of no use to her."

Law was momentarily staggered, but he recovered himself. "She would know I was doing for myself," he said, "which might mean something for her, too, in time. I might send for her. At least," said the lad, "she would not have me on her hands; she would only have herself to think of; and if she got on in her singing—the fact is, I can't stand it, and one way or other I must get away."

"What would you do if you were in Australia, Law?"

"Hang it all!" said the young man, tears of vexation and despite starting to his eyes, "a fellow must be good for something somewhere. You can't be useless all round; I'm strong enough. And here's one thing I've found out," Law added with a laugh: "it doesn't go against your pride to do things in the Colonies which you durstn't do here. You can do—whatever you *can* do out there. It doesn't matter being a gentleman. A gentleman can drive a cart or carry a load in Australia. That is the kind of place for me. I'd do whatever turned up."

Said Mr. Ashford suddenly, "I know a man out there—" and then he paused. "Law, what would your sister do? There would be no one to stand by her. Even you, you have not much in your power, but you are always some one. You can give her a little sympathy. Even to feel that there are two of you must be something."

"Mr. Ashford," said Law, "you will do her more good than I should. What have I been to poor Lottie? Only a trouble. Two of us—no; I can't take even that to myself. I've worried her more than anything else. She would be the first to thank you. You know a man—?"

"I know a man," said the Minor Canon—"I had forgotten him till now—a man who owes me a good turn; and I think he would pay it. If I were sure you would really do your best, and not forget the claims she has upon your kindness—"

"Would you like me to send for her as soon as I had a home for her?" Law asked with fervour. There was a subdued twinkle in his eye, but yet he was too much in earnest not to be ready to make any promise.

"That would be the right thing to do," said the Minor Canon with excessive gravity, "though perhaps the bush is not exactly the kind of place to suit her. If you will promise to do your very best—"

"I will," said the lad, "I will. I am desperate otherwise; you can see for yourself, Mr. Ashford. Give me only an opening; give me anything that I can work at. If I were to 'list I never should make much money by that. There's only just this one thing," said Law: "If I had a friend to go to, and a chance of employment, and would promise to pay it back, I suppose I might get a loan somewhere—a loan on good interest," he continued, growing anxious and a little breathless—"perhaps from one of those societies, or some old money-lender, or something—to take me out?"

The Minor Canon laughed. "If this is what you are really set upon, and you will do your best," he said, "I will see your father, and you need not trouble your mind about the interest. Perhaps we shall be able to manage that."

"Oh, Mr. Ashford, what a good fellow you are! what a good friend you are!" cried Law, beaming with happiness. The tears once more came into his eyes, and then there came a glow of suppressed malice and fun behind that moisture. "Lottie will be more obliged even than I," he said; "and I could send for her as soon as I got settled out there."

CHAPTER XXXVIII
LOTTIE RESENTFUL

Lottie was sadly disheartened by the events of that day. She came home alike depressed and indignant, her heart and her pride equally wounded. She had scarcely seen Rollo for the two intervening days, and the meeting at the Signor's had appeared to her before it came a piece of happiness which was certain, and with which no one could interfere. He would resist all attempts to wile him away for that afternoon, she was sure; he would not disappoint her and take all her inspiration from her again. Since that last meeting under the elm-tree she had been more full of happy confidence in him than ever. His readiness and eagerness to take her away at once, overcoming, as she thought, all the scruples and prejudices of his class, in order to secure deliverance for her, had filled her mind with that soft glow of gratitude which it is so sweet to feel to those we love. The elation and buoyant sense of happiness in her mind had floated her over all the lesser evils in her path. What did they matter, what did anything matter, in comparison? She was magnanimous, tolerant, ready to believe the best, unready to be offended, because of this private solace of happiness in her bosom, but all the more for those undoubting certainties she had felt the contrast of the actual scene. She did not even think that Rollo might be innocent of his cousin's visit, or that he knew nothing of her coming till he had walked unawares into the snare. Lottie did not know this. She saw him by Augusta's side, talking to her and listening to her. She was conscious through all her being of the rustle of whispering behind her, which went on in spite of her singing. She would not look at him to see what piteous apologies he was making with his eyes, and when Mrs. O'Shaughnessy in sudden wrath dragged her away Lottie was glad of the sudden exit, the little demonstration of offence and independence of which she herself might have failed to take the initiative. She went home tingling with the wound, her nerves excited, her mind irritated. She would not go to meet him, as he had asked her. She went home instead, avoiding everybody, and shut herself up in her own room. She was discouraged too and deeply annoyed with herself, because in the presence of the unkindly critic who had been listening to her, Lottie felt she had not done well. Generally her only care, her only thought, was to please Rollo; but that day she would have wished for the inspiring power that now and then came upon her, as when she had sung in the Abbey not knowing of his presence. She would have liked to sing like that, overawing Augusta and her whispering; but she had not done so. She had failed while that semi-friend who was her enemy looked on. She felt, with a subtle certainty beyond all need of proof, that Augusta was her enemy. Augusta had at once suspected, though Rollo had said that she would never suspect; and she wanted to make her cousin see how little Lottie was his equal, how even in her best gifts she was nothing. It was bitter to Lottie to think that she had done all she could to prove Augusta right. Why was it that she could not sing then, as, two or three times in her life, she had felt able to sing, confounding all who had been unfavourable to her? Lottie chafed at the failure she had made. She was angry with herself, and this made her more angry both with Augusta and with him. In the heat of her self-resentment she began to sing over her music softly to herself, noting where she had failed. Had the Signor been within hearing how he would have rejoiced over that self-instruction. Her friends had been so much mortified that it opened her eyes to her own faults. She saw where she had been wrong. There is no such stimulant of excellence as the sense of having done badly. Lottie's art education advanced under the sting of this failure as it had never done before. She threw herself into it with fervour. As she ran over the notes she seemed to hear the "sibilant s's" behind her, pursuing her, and the chance words she had caught. "Like him—she did not care a straw for him." "The old lady made it all up," "and the settlements were astonishing." That and a great deal more Lottie's jealous ears had picked up, almost against her will, and the words goaded her on like so many pricks. She thought she never could suffer it to be possible that Augusta or any other fine lady should do less than listen when she sang again.

While Lottie sat there cold in the wintry twilight (yet warm with injured pride and mortification) till there was scarcely light enough to see, humming over her music, Rollo, getting himself with difficulty free of his cousin and all the visitors and commotion of the Deanery, rushed up to the elm-tree, and spent a very uncomfortable moment there, waiting in the cold, and wondering if it was possible that she would not come. It did not occur to him that Lottie, always so acquiescent and persuadable, could stand out now, especially as he was not really to blame. He stood about under the elm, now and then taking a little walk up and down to keep himself warm, watching the light steal out of the wide landscape and everything darken round him, for half and hour and more. No one was there; not an old Chevalier ventured upon a turn in the dark, not a pair of lovers confronted the north wind. Rollo shivered, though he was more warmly clad than Lottie would have been. He walked up and down with an impatience that helped to keep him warm, though with dismay that neutralised that livelier feeling. He had no desire to lose his love in this way. It might be foolish to imperil his comfort, his position, his very living, for her, but yet now at least Rollo had no intention of throwing her away. He knew why she sang badly that afternoon, and instead of alarming him this knowledge brought a smile upon his face. Augusta had behaved like a woman without a heart, and Lottie was no tame girl to bear whatever anyone pleased, but a creature full of fire and spirit, not to be crushed by a fashionable persecutor. Rollo felt it hard that he should wait in the cold, and be disappointed after all; but he was not angry with Lottie. She had a right to be displeased. He was all the more anxious not to lose her, not to let her get free from him, that she had thus asserted herself. His love, which had been a little blown about by those fashionable gales that had been blowing round him, blazed up all the hotter for this temporary restraint put upon it. She who had trusted him with such an exquisite trust only the other evening, who had not in her innocence seen anything but devotion in the sudden proposal into which (he persuaded himself) only passion could have hurried him—her first rebellion against him tightened the ties that bound him to her. Give her up! it would be giving up heaven, throwing away the sweetest thing in his life. He was cold, but his heart burned as he paced his little round, facing the north wind and listening for every rustling sound among the withered leaves that lay around him, thinking it might be her step. The darkness, and the chill, and the solitude all seemed to show him more clearly how sweet the intercourse had been which had made him unconscious of either darkness or cold before. Augusta repeating her endless monotonous stories of universal guile and selfishness had made him half ashamed of his best feelings. He was ashamed now of her and her influence, ashamed of having been made her tool for the humiliation of his love. What a difference there was between them! Was there anyone else in the world so tender, so pure, so exquisite in her love and trust, as Lottie, the creature whose sensitive heart he had been made to wound? When at last, discouraged and penitent, he turned homeward, Rollo had the intention trembling in his mind of making Lottie the most complete amends for everything that had ever been done to harm her. He paused at the gates of the cloister, and looked across at the light in her window with a yearning which surprised him. He seemed to have a thousand things to say to her, and to be but half a being when he had not her to confide in, to tell all his affairs to—although he had never told her one of his affairs. This fact did not seem to affect his longing. He went so far as to walk across the Dean's Walk, to see what he thought was her shadow on the blind. It was not Lottie's shadow, but Polly's, who had taken her place; but this the lover did not know.

Meanwhile Lottie had been disturbed in her seclusion by a sharp knock at her door. "Do you mean to stay there all night, Miss?" cried Polly's sharp voice. "You might pay me the compliment to keep me company now and again as long as you stay in my house. If you think it is civil to stay there, shut up in your room, and me all alone in the drawing-room, I don't. I can't think where your hearts is, you two," Polly went on, a whimper breaking into the tone of offence with which she spoke. "To see one as is not much older than yourself, and never did you no harm, and not a soul to keep her company. Was it for that I give up all my own folks, to come and sit dressed up in a corner because I'm Mrs. Despard, and never see a soul?"

Lottie had opened her door before this speech was half done. She said with a little alarm, "Please don't speak so loud. We need not let the maid in the kitchen know."

"Do you think I care for the maid in the kitchen? She's my servant. I'll make her know her place. Never one of them sort of folks takes any freedom with me. I have always been known for one as allowed no freedoms—no, nor no followers, nor perquisites, nor nothing of the kind. They soon find out as I ain't one to be turned round their finger. Now you," said Polly, leading the way into the little drawing-room, "you're one of the soft sort. I dare say they did what they liked with you!"

"I don't think so," said Lottie, following. She put her music softly down upon the old piano, which Polly had swathed in a cover, and the changed aspect of the room moved her half to laughter, half to anger and dismay.

"There are few as knows themselves," said Polly. "That girl, that Mary as you had, I couldn't have put up with her for a day. Some folks never sees when things is huggermugger, but I'm very particular. Your Pa—dear, good, easy man—I dare say he's put up with a deal; but to be sure no better was to be expected, for you never had no training, I suppose?"

Lottie was almost too much taken by surprise to reply—she, who had felt that if there was one thing in the world she could do it was house-keeping! The confusion that is produced in the mind by the sudden perception of another's opinion of us which is diametrically opposed to our own seized her; otherwise she would have been roused to instant wrath. This, which was something so entirely opposite to what she could have expected, raised only a kind of ludicrous bewilderment in her mind. "I—don't know what you mean," said Lottie. "Papa has not very much money to give for house-keeping. Perhaps you are making a mistake."

"Oh, it is likely that I should make a mistake! Do you think I don't know my own husband's income? Do you think," said Polly with scorn, "that he has any secrets from *me*?"

Lottie was cold with her imprisonment in her fireless room. She drew her little chair to the blazing fire and sat down by the side. Polly had placed herself in the largest chair in the room, directly in front of it. The fire was heaped up in the little grate, and blazed, being largely supplied. It was very comfortable, but it went against the rules of the economy which Lottie had strenuously prescribed to herself. "Papa spends a great deal of money himself," she said; "you will find that you must be very sparing at home."

"My dear," said Polly in a tone of condescending patronage which brought the colour to Lottie's face, "I am not one as can be sparing at home. Pinching ain't my way. I couldn't do it, not if I was to be made a countess for it. Some folks can scrape and cut down and look after everything, but it ain't my nature. What I like is a free hand. Plenty to eat and plenty to drink, and no stinting nowhere—that's what will always be the law in my house."

Lottie made no reply. She felt that it was almost a failure from her duty to put out her hands to the warmth of the too beautiful fire. Some one would have to suffer for it. Her mind began to run over her own budget of ways and means, to try, as had been her old habit, where she could find something to cut off to make up for the extravagance. "These coals burn very fast," she said at last. "They are not a thrifty kind. I used to have the—"

"I know," said Polly, "you used to have slates and think it was economy—poor child!—but the best for me: the best is always the cheapest in the end. If anyone thinks as I will put up with seconds, either coals or bread!—but since we're on the subject of money," continued Polly, "I'll tell you my mind, Miss, and I don't mean it unfriendly. The thing as eats up my husband's money, it ain't a bright fire or a good dinner, as is his right to have; it's your brother Law, Miss, and you."

"You have told me that before," Lottie said, with a strenuous effort at self-control.

"And I'll tell it you again—and again—till it has its effect," cried Polly: "it's true. I don't mean to be unfriendly. I wonder how you can live upon your Pa at your age. Why, long before I was your age I was doing for myself. My Pa was very respectable, and everybody belonging to us; but do you think I'd have stayed at home and eat up what the old folks had for themselves? They'd have kept me and welcome, but I wouldn't hear of it. And do you mean to say," said Polly, folding her arms and fixing her eyes upon her step-daughter, "as you think yourself better than me?"

Lottie returned the stare with glowing eyes, her lips falling apart from very wonder. She gave a kind of gasp of bewilderment, but made no reply.

"I don't suppose as you'll say so," said Polly; "and why shouldn't you think of your family as I did of mine? You mightn't be able to work as I did, but there's always things you could do to save your Pa a little money. There's lessons. There's nothing ungenteel in lessons. I am not one as would be hard upon a girl just starting in the world. You've got your room here, that don't cost you nothing; and what's a daily governess's work? Nothing to speak of—two or three hours' teaching (or you might as well call it playing), and your dinner with the children, and mostly with the lady of the house—and all the comforts of 'ome after, just as if you wasn't out in the world at all; a deal different from sitting at your needle, working, working, as I've done, from morning to night."

"But I don't know anything," said Lottie. "I almost think you are quite right. Perhaps it is all true; it doesn't matter nowadays, and ladies ought to work as well as men. But—I don't know anything." A half-smile came over her face. Notwithstanding that she was angry with Rollo, still—he who would have carried her away on the spot rather than that she should bear the shadow of a humiliation at home—was it likely—? Lottie's mind suddenly leaped out of its anger and resentment with a sudden rebound. He did not deserve that she should be so angry with him. Was it his fault? and in forgiving him her temper and her heart got suddenly right again, and all was well. She even woke to a little amusement in the consciousness that Polly was advising her for her good. The extravagant coals, the extravagant meals, would soon bring their own punishment; and though Lottie could not quite free herself from irritation on these points, yet she was amused by the thought of all this good advice.

"That's nonsense," said Polly promptly. "Now here's a way you could begin at once, and it would be practice for you, and it would show at least that you was willing. I've been very careless," she said, getting up from her chair and opening the old piano. She had to push off the cover first, and the noise and commotion of this complicated movement filled Lottie with alarm. "I've done as a many young ladies do before they see how silly it is. I've left off my music. You mayn't believe it, but it's true. I can't tell even if I know my notes," said Polly, jauntily but clumsily placing her hands upon the keyboard and letting one finger fall heavily here and there like a hammer. "I don't remember a bit. It's just like a great silly, isn't it? But you never think when you are young, when your head's full of your young man and all that sort of thing. It's when you've settled down, and got married, and have time to think, that you find it out."

Polly was a great deal less careful of her language as she became accustomed to her new surroundings. She was fully herself by this time, and at her ease. She sat down before the piano and ran her finger along the notes. "It's scandalous," she said. "We're taught when we're young, and then we thinks no more of it. Now, Miss, if you was willing to do something for your living, if you was really well disposed and wanted to make a return, you might just look up some of your old lesson-books and begin with me. I'd soon pick up," said Polly, making a run of sound up and down the keys with the back of her fingers, and thinking it beautiful; "it would come back to me in two or three lessons. You needn't explain nothing about it; we might just say as we were learning some duets together. It would all come back to me if you would take a little trouble; and I shouldn't forget it. I never forget it when anyone's of use to me."

"But," cried Lottie, who had been vainly endeavouring to break in, "I cannot play."

"Cannot play!" Polly turned round upon the piano-stool with a countenance of horror. Even to turn round upon that stool was something delightful to her, like a lady in a book, like one of the heroines in the *Family Herald*; but this intimation chilled the current of her blood.

"No—only two or three little things, and that chiefly by ear. I never learned as I ought. I hated it; and I was scarcely ever taught, only by—someone who did not know much," said Lottie with a compunction in her mind. Only by someone who did not know much—This was her mother, poor soul, whom Polly had replaced. Lottie's heart swelled as she spoke. Poor, kind, silly mamma! she had not known very much; but it seemed cruel to allow it in the presence of her supplanter.

"Goodness—gracious—me!" said Polly. She said each word separately, as if she were telling beads. She cast at Lottie a glance of sovereign contempt. "You to set up for being a lady," she cried, "and can't *play the piano*! I never heard of such a thing in all my born days."

If she had claimed not to be able to work, Polly could have understood it; but if there is a badge of ladyhood, or even a pretence at ladyhood, in the world, is it not this? She was horrified; it felt like a coming down in the world even to Polly herself.

Again Lottie did not make any reply. She was simple enough to be half ashamed of herself and half angry at the criticism which for the first time touched her; for it was a fact that she was ignorant, and a shameful fact. She could not defend, but she would not excuse herself. As for Polly, there was in her a mingling of triumph and regret.

"I *am* surprised," she said. "I thought one who pretended to be a lady ought at least to know that much. And you ought to be a lady, I am sure, if ever anyone was, for your Pa is a perfect gentleman. Dear, dear—if you can't play the piano, goodness gracious, what have you been doing all your life? That was the one thing I thought was sure—and you are musical, for I've heard as you could sing. If it's only that you won't take any trouble to oblige," said Polly angrily, "say it out. Oh, it won't be no surprise to me. I've seen it in your face already—say it out!"

"I have told you nothing but the truth," said Lottie. "I am sorry for it. I can sing—a little—but I can't play."

"It's just the same as if you said you could write but couldn't read," said Polly; "but I've always been told as I've a nice voice. It ain't your loud kind, that you could hear from this to the Abbey, but sweet—at least so folks say. You can teach me to sing if you like," she said, after a pause. "I never learned singing. One will do as well as the other, and easier too."

This was a still more desperate suggestion. Lottie quailed before the task that was offered to her. "I can show you the scales," she said doubtfully; "that is the beginning of everything; but singing is harder to teach than playing. The Signor thinks I don't know anything. They say I have a voice, but that I don't know how to sing."

"The fact is," cried Polly, shutting down the piano with a loud bang and jar which made the whole instrument thrill, and snapped an old attenuated chord which went out of existence with a creak and a groan, "the fact is, you don't want to do nothing for me. You don't think me good enough for you. I am only your father's wife, and one as has a claim upon your respect, and deserves to have the best you can do. If it was one of your fine ladies as don't care a brass farthing for you—oh, you'd sing and you'd play the piano safe enough: but you've set your mind against me. I seen it the first day I came here—and since then the life you've led me! Never a civil word—never a pleasant look; yes and no, with never a turn of your head; you think a deal of yourself. And you needn't suppose I care—not I—not one bit; but you shan't stand up to my face and refuse whatever I ask you. You'll have to do what I tell you or you'll have to go."

"I will go," said Lottie in a low voice. She thought of Rollo's sudden proposal, of the good people whom he said he would take her to, of the sudden relief and hope, the peace and ease that were involved. Ought she not to take him at his word? For the moment she thought she would do so. She would let him know that she was ready, ready to go anywhere, only to escape from this. How foolish she had been to be angry with Rollo—he who wanted nothing better than to deliver her at a stroke, to carry her away into happiness. Her heart softened with a great gush of tenderness. She would yield to him; why should she not yield to him? She might think that he ought to marry his wife from her father's house, but he had not seemed to think so. He thought of nothing but to deliver her from this humiliation—and what would it matter to him? a poor Chevalier's house or a poor quiet lodging, what would it matter? She would go. She would do as Rollo said.

"You will go?" cried Polly; "and where will you go? Who have you got to take you in? People ain't so fond of you. A woman as can do nothing for herself, who wants her? and isn't even obliging. Oh, you are going to your room again, to be sulky there? But I tell you I won't have it. You shall sit where the family sits or you shall go out of the place altogether. And you'll come to your meals like other people, and you'll mix with them as is there, and not set up your white face, as if you were better than all the world. You're not so grand as you think you are, Miss Lottie Despard. If it comes to that I'm a Despard as well as you; and I'm a married woman, with an 'usband to work for me—an 'usband," cried Polly, "as doesn't require to work for me, as has enough to keep me like a lady—if it wasn't that he has a set of lazy grown-up children as won't do nothing for themselves, but eat us out of 'ouse and 'ome!"

Was it possible that this humiliation had come to Lottie—to Lottie of all people—she who had felt that the well-being of the house hung upon her, and that she alone stood between her family and utter downfall? She sat still, not even attempting now to escape, her ears tingling, her heart beating. It was incredible that it was she, her very self, Lottie, who was bearing this. It must be a dream; it was impossible that it could be true.

And thus Lottie sat the whole of the evening, too proud to withdraw, and bore the brunt of a long series of attacks, which were interrupted, indeed, by the supper, to which Polly had to give some personal care, and by Captain Despard's entrance and Law's. Polly told her story to her husband with indignant vehemence. "I asked her," she said, "to help me a bit with my music—I know you're fond of music, Harry—and I thought we'd learn up some duets or something, her and me, to please you; and she says she can't play the piano! and, then, not to show no offence, I said as singing would do just as well, and then she says she can't sing!" The Captain received this statement with much caressing of his wife and smoothing of her ruffled plumes. He said, "Lottie, another time you'll pay more attention," with a severe aspect; and not even Law had a word to say in her defence. As to Law, indeed, he was very much preoccupied with his own affairs; his eyes were shining, his face full of secret importance and meaning. Lottie saw that he was eager to catch her eye, but she did not understand the telegraphic communications he addressed to her. Nor did she understand him much better when he pulled her sleeve and whispered, "I am going to Australia," when the tedious evening was over. Law's career had fallen out of her thoughts in the troubles of those few weeks past. She had even ceased to ask how he was getting on, or take any interest in his books; she remembered this with a pang when she found herself at last safe in the shelter of her room. She had given up one part of her natural duty when the other was taken from her. Australia? What could he mean? She thought she would question him to-morrow; but to-morrow brought her another series of petty struggles, and once more concentrated her mind upon her own affairs.

CHAPTER XXXIX
LOTTIE SUBDUED

"I waited half an hour. I was not very happy," said Rollo. "It is never cold when you are here, but last night the wind went through and through me. That is the consequence of being alone. And you, my Lottie, had you no compunctions? Could you make yourself happy without any thought of the poor fellow freezing under the elm-tree?"

"Happy!" Lottie cried. She was happy now. Last night she had been alone, no one in the world caring what became of her; now she felt safe, as if the world held nothing but friends; but she shivered, notwithstanding her lover's supporting arm.

"Not happy then? Does it not answer, darling? Can you endure the woman? Is she better than at first? I like her," said Rollo, "for you know it was her arrival which opened your heart to me—which broke the ice—which brought us together. I shall always feel charitably towards her for that."

Lottie shivered again. "No, it is not because of the cold," she said. "I do not suppose you could understand if I were to tell you. Home! I have not any home!" cried the girl. "I was thinking—if it was really true what you said the other night—if it would make no difference to you, Rollo, to take your wife out of some poor little lodging instead of out of her father's house—are you sure you would not mind?" she said, looking wistfully, anxiously into his face. In the waning light all he could see distinctly was this wistful dilation of her eyes, gazing intently to read, before he could utter it, his answer in his face. "I could manage to live somehow," she went on, tremulously. "Though I cannot give lessons, I can work, very well. I think I am almost sure I could get work. No; I would not take money from you; I could not, Rollo:—not until—no, no; that would be quite impossible; rather stay here and bear it all than that. But if really, truly, to marry a poor girl, living in a poor little room, working for her bread, would not make any difference to you—. Oh, I know, I know it is not what ought to be—even here, even at home, I am not equal to you. You ought to have some one a great deal better off—a great deal higher in the world. But if you would not think it—discreditable; if you would not be ashamed— oh, Rollo," she cried,

"I cannot bear it! it is impossible to bear it!—I would ask you to do what you offered and take me away!"

It is impossible to describe the feelings with which Rollo listened to these unexpected words. To see a bird walk into the snare must awake compunctions in the most experienced trapper. The same sensation does not attend a sudden fall; but the sight of an innocent creature going calmly into the death set before it, as if into safety and shelter—a man must be hard indeed to see that unmoved. And Rollo was no villain. His heart gave one wild leap again, as it had done when, in the hurrying of passion, not with deliberation (as he had always been comforted to think), he had laid that snare. The thrill of his hairbreadth escape from her horror and loathing, the leap of sudden, horrified delight to find her in his power all at once, by her own act and deed, transported him for the moment with almost uncontrollable power; and then this sudden passion in his mind was met by the stream, the torrent, of a more generous impulse, a nobler passion, which carried everything before it. A man may trap his prey with guile, he may take advantage of the half-willingness of a frail resistance; but to turn to shame the perfect and tender confidence of innocence, who but a villain could do that? and Rollo was no villain. He grasped her almost convulsively in his arms as she spoke; he tried to interrupt her, the words surging, almost incoherent, to his lips. "Lottie! my Lottie!" he cried, "this is not how it must be. Do you think I will let you go to live alone, to work, as you say?" He took her hand hastily, and kissed the little cold fingers with lips that trembled. "No, my love, my darling, not that—but I will go to town to-morrow and settle how we can be married—at once, without an hour's delay. Oh, yes, it is possible, dear—quite possible. It is the only thing to do. Why, why did I not think of it before? I will go and settle everything, and get the licence. That is the way. My darling, you must not say a word. You had made up your mind to marry me some time, and why not to-morrow—next day—as soon as I can settle? What should we wait for? who should we think of except ourselves? And I want you, my love; and you, thank heaven, Lottie, have need of me."

He held her close to him, in a grasp which was almost fierce—fierce in the strain of virtue and honour, in which his own nature, with all its easy principles and vacillations, was caught too. He wanted to be off and do it at once, without losing a moment, lest his heart should fail. He would do it, whatever might oppose. She should never know that less worthy thoughts had been in his mind. She should find that her trust was not vain. His blood ran in his veins like a tumultuous river, and his heart beat so that Lottie herself was overawed by the commotion as he held her against it. She was half frightened by his vehemence and tried to speak, but he would not let her at first. "No," he said, "no, you must not say anything. You must not oppose me. It must be done first, and then we can think of it after. There is nothing against it, and everything in its favour. You must not say a word but Yes," he cried.

"But, Rollo, Rollo, let me speak. It might be good for me, but would it not be wrong for you? Oh, let me speak! Am I so selfish that I would make you take a sudden resolution, perhaps very foolish, perhaps very imprudent, for my sake? Rollo, Rollo, don't! I will bear anything. It would be wrong for you to do this."

"No; not wrong, but right—not wrong, but right," he cried, bewildering her with his vehemence. Lottie's own heart was stirred, but not like this. She wondered and was troubled, even in the delight of the thought that everything in the world was as nothing to him in comparison with his love for herself.

"But, Rollo," she cried again, trembling in his grasp, "if this is really possible—if it is not wrong—why should you go to London to do it? It would be quite as easy here—"

"Lottie, you will sacrifice something for me, will you not?" he said. "If it were done here, all would be public; it would be spoken of everywhere; and I want it to be quiet. I have not much money. You will make this sacrifice for me, dear—"

"Oh," said Lottie, compunctious, "I wish I had said nothing about it; I wish I had not disturbed you with my paltry little troubles. Do not think of them any more. I can bear anything when I know you are thinking of me. It was only yesterday when—when all seemed uncertain, that it seemed more than I could bear."

"And it is more than you ought to bear," he said. "No, I am glad that you told me. We will go away, Lottie—to Italy, to the sunshine, to the country of music, where you will learn best of all—we will go away from the very church door."

And then he told her how it could be done. To-morrow he would go and settle everything. His plans all took form with lightning speed, though he had never thought of them till now. There would be many things to do; but in three days from that time he would meet her in the same place, and tell her all the arrangements he had made:—and the next morning after that ("Saturday is a lucky day," he said) they would go to town, if not together, yet by the same train—and go to the church, where he would have arranged everything. Rollo Ridsdale was an adventurer born. He was used to changing the conditions of his life in a moment, in the twinkling of an eye. But it all seemed a dream to Lottie—not one of her usual waking dreams, but a dream of the night, with no possibility in it, which would dissolve into the mists presently and leave nothing but a happy recollection.

She acquiesced in everything, being too much taken by surprise to oppose a plan in which he was so vehement.

"May I tell Law?" she asked, always in her dream, not feeling as if there was any reality in the idea she suggested. And he said No at first, but afterwards half relented, and it was agreed that on Friday everything was to be decided, but nothing done till then. Thus, though they had met without a thought that this stolen interview would be more decisive than any other of the same kind, they parted with a decision that concerned their entire lives.

They walked closer together after this, in the safe gloom of the darkness, till they had again reached the door of the cloisters which led to the Deanery. No one was about, and Rollo was full of restless excitement. He would not hear what she said about prudence, and walked across with her to her own door. There was not a creature to be seen up or down; the lamps flickered in the cold wind, and all the population had gone in to the comfort of warm rooms and blazing fires. He kissed her hand tenderly as he took leave of her.

"Till Friday," he said.

Lottie went in, still in her dream, walking, she thought, in her sleep. She hoped this sleep would last for ever—that it might not be rashly disturbed by waking, or even by that which would be almost as bad as waking—*coming true*. She could scarcely feel that she wanted it to come true; it was enough as it was, a bewildering happiness that tingled to the very ends of her fingers, that made her feel as if she were walking on air. She went softly upstairs, caring for nothing but to get to her room, where, though it was dark and cold, she could still go on with this wonderful vision. That seemed all she wanted. But, alas! something very different was in store for Lottie. As she went with soft steps up the stairs the door of the little drawing-room was suddenly opened, letting out a warm stream of ruddy light. Then a sound of laughter reached her ears, and Polly's voice—

"Come in, come in; we are waiting for you; we are both here," with another gay outburst.

Lottie came to herself, and to all the disagreeable realities of her life, with a start of pain. She had to obey, though nothing could be more disagreeable to her. She went in with dazzled eyes into the room full of firelight. She remembered now that she had remarked outside that no lamp was lighted, and had supposed with relief that Mrs. Despard was out. But Mrs. Despard had not been out. She had been lurking in the ruddy gloom near the window, her husband by her side. They greeted Lottie with another laugh, as she came in with her pale, astonished face within the circle of the fire.

"So that's how you spend your afternoons, miss, as I never could think where you were," cried Polly; "but why didn't you bring in your beau with you? I'd have given him his tea and a nice leg of a goose, as comfortable as could be."

"My child," said the Captain on his side, "I congratulate you. I've been expecting something of this kind for a long time. I've had my eye upon you. But why didn't you bring Mr. Ridsdale in, as Mrs. Despard says?"

Lottie felt as if she had been turned into stone. She stood all dark in her winter dress, the firelight playing upon her, and seeking in vain to catch at some possibility of reflection. She had not even a button that would give back the light. And she had not a word to say.

"Come, come, you need not be so put out," said the Captain, not unkindly. "We saw you coming; and very proper of Mr. Ridsdale not to leave you at the Deanery, but to see you home to your own door. You thought no one was paying any attention—but I hope," Captain Despard added, "that I think more than that of my child. I don't doubt from what I saw, Lottie, that you understand each other; and why hasn't he come before now to speak to me? You might have known that such a suitor would not be received unfavourably. Happy myself," said the Captain, throwing out his chest, "would I have put any obstacle between you and your happiness, my dear?"

"I did not think—I did not know—I think—you are mistaken," Lottie faltered, not knowing what to say.

"Mistaken, indeed! Oh, we've gone through all that too lately to be mistaken, haven't we, Harry?" cried Mrs. Despard. "We know all about it. You couldn't come to those as would understand you better. Don't be frightened; you haven't been found out in anything wrong. If that was wrong I've a deal to answer for," Polly cried, laughing. "I should think you must be frozen with cold after wandering about on them Slopes, or wherever you have been. How foolish young people are, to be sure, getting their deaths of cold. We never were as foolish as that, were we, Harry? Come and warm yourself, you silly girl. You needn't be afraid of him or me."

Amid their laughter, however, Lottie managed to get away, to take off her hat, and to try as best she could to realise this new phase of the situation. What her father had said was very reasonable. Why had not Rollo come, as the Captain said? How that would have simplified everything, made everything legitimate! She sighed, not able to understand her lover, feeling that for once her father was right; but Rollo had said that this could not be, that it would be necessary to keep everything quiet. Her dream of happiness was disturbed. Dreams are better, so much better, than reality. In them there is never any jar with fact and necessity; they can adapt themselves to everything, fit themselves into every new development. But now that she was fully awoke it was less easy to steer her way through all the obstacles.

Rollo's reluctance to declare himself, and her father's right to know, and the pain of leaving her home in a clandestine way, all rushed upon her, dispersing her happiness to the winds. She had felt that to awake would be to lose the sweetness which had wrapped her about; and now the rude encounter with the world had come, and Lottie felt that even with that prospect of happiness before her it was difficult to bear what she would have to bear;—Polly's innuendoes and, worse still, Polly's sympathy, and the questions of her father appalled her as she looked forward to them. During this strange courtship of hers, so perplexed and mixed up as it was with her music and the "career" which they all, even Rollo, had tried to force upon her (though surely there need be no more of that *now*), and the changes that had taken place at home, Lottie had almost lost herself. She was no longer the high-spirited girl, full of energy and strength, who had reigned over this little house and dragged Law's heavy bulk along through so many difficulties. She had dreamed so much, and taken refuge so completely from the troubles of her position in those dreams, that now she seemed to have lost her own characteristics, and had no vigour to sustain her when she had actual difficulties to face. She tried to recall herself to herself as she smoothed her hair, which had been blown about by the breeze. From the beginning she had been pained by Rollo's reserve, though she had persuaded herself it was natural enough; but now, in this new, strange revolution of affairs—a revolution caused entirely, she said to herself, by her father's own proceedings—what could she do but stand firm on her own side? She would not betray the great purpose in hand. She would still her own heart, and keep her composure, and not allow any agitation or any irritation to wrest from her the secret which Rollo desired to keep. To smooth her ruffled hair was not generally a long process with Lottie; but it was more difficult to arrange her agitated thoughts, and there had been various calls for her from below, where the others had gone for their evening meal, before she was ready to follow.

Finally Law was sent upstairs with an urgent demand for her presence.

"They've gone to tea," said Law, knocking at her door; and then he added, in a low tone, "Open, Lottie. I want to speak to you. I have got lots to say to you."

She heard him, but she did not attach any meaning to his words. What he said to her on the night before had left no definite impression on her mind. Law had lost his sister, who thought of him above all. In the midst of a pressing crisis in our own individual life, which of us has time to think of others? She was afraid to talk to Law, afraid to betray herself. Love made Lottie selfish and self-absorbed, a consequence just as apt to follow as any other. She was afraid of betraying herself to him; her mind was too full of this wonderful revolution in her own life to be able to take in Law's desire, on his side, not to know about her, but to expound himself. She came out upon him hastily, and brushed past him, saying, "I am ready." She did not think of Law, not even when he followed her, grumbling and murmuring—"I told you I wanted to speak to you." How difficult it is to realise the wants of another when one's heart is full of one's own concerns! Neither brother nor sister had room in their minds for anything but the momentous event in their respective lives which was coming; but Law was aggrieved, for he had always hitherto possessed Lottie's sympathy as a chattel of his own.

Polly and the Captain were seated at table when the two younger members of the family went in, and never had Captain Despard been more dignified or genial. "Lottie, my child, a bit of the breast," he said—"a delicate bit just fit for a lady. I've saved it up for you, though you are late. You are very late; but for once in a way we will make allowances, especially as Mrs. Despard is not offended, but takes your side."

"Oh, *I* know," said Polly, "I am not one as is hard upon natural feelings. Pride I can't abide, nor stuck-up ways, but when it comes to keeping company—"

"Is anyone keeping company with Lottie?" said Law, looking up fiercely; and then the elder pair laughed.

"But, my love, it is not a phrase that is used in good society," the Captain said.

"Oh, bother good society!" said Polly. She was in an exuberant mood, and beyond the influence of that little topdressing of too transparent pretence with which occasionally she attempted to impose upon her step-children. Lottie, in whose mind indignation and disgust gradually overcame the previous self-absorption, listened to every word, unable to escape from the chatter she hated, with that keen interest of dislike and impatience which is more enthralling than affection; but she scarcely ventured to raise her eyes, and kept herself rigidly on her guard lest any rash word should betray her. It was not till the meal was over that she was brought to actual proof. Then her father detained her as she was about to escape. Law, more impatient than ever with the pressure of his own affairs, which it seemed impossible to find any opportunity of confiding to his sister, had got up at once and gone out. The Captain threw out his chest majestically and waved his hand as Lottie was about to follow.

"My child, I have got something to say to you," he said.

Mrs. Despard was standing by the fire, warming herself with frank ease, with a good ankle well displayed. Lottie, on her way to the door, unwillingly arrested, stood still because she could not help it. But the Captain occupied with majesty his seat at the foot of the table between his wife and his daughter. "My love," he said, with his favourite gesture, throwing back his well-developed shoulders, "I have every faith in my daughter, and Mr. Ridsdale is in every way quite satisfactory. Your family is as good as his, but my Lord Courtland's son is not one to be turned away from any door; and as you have no fortune, Lottie, I should not be exacting as to settlements. I suppose he knows that you have no fortune, my dear?"

"La, Harry!" said Polly from the side of the fire, "how should he think she had a fortune? Fortunes don't grow on every tree. And how do you know as he has got *that* far? A young man may keep company with a girl for long enough, and yet never go as far as *that*."

"You must allow me to know best, my love," said the Captain. "I hope he is not trifling with my girl's affections. If he is he has Harry Despard to deal with, I'd have him to know. By Jove, if I thought *that*!"

"I dare say it's nothing but keeping company," said Polly, holding up her foot to the fire. "Taking a walk together, or a talk; there's nothing wrong in that. She wants her bit of fun as well as other girls. I'm not the one to stand up for Miss Lottie, for it's not what she'd do for me; but if it's only her bit of fun you shouldn't be hard upon her, Harry; if my pa had hauled me up for that—"

Lottie could not bear it any longer. "Do you wish me to stay," she said, "papa? can you wish me to stay?" The Captain looked from his wife in her easy attitude to his daughter, pale with indignation and horror.

"My love," he said, with mild remonstrance, "there are different ways of speaking in different spheres. Lottie is an only daughter, and has been very carefully brought up. But, my child," the Captain added, turning to Lottie, "you must not be neglected now. I will make it my business to-morrow to see Mr. Ridsdale, to ascertain what his intentions are. Your interests shall not suffer from any carelessness."

"Papa," cried Lottie in despair, "you will not do anything so cruel; you could not treat me so! Wait—only wait—a few days—three or four days!"

Polly was so much interested that she let her dress drop over her ankles and turned round. "Don't you see," she said, "that she feels he's coming to the point without any bother? That's always a deal the best way. It can't do no harm, as I can see, to wait for three or four days."

"By Jove, but it will, though," said Captain Despard with sudden impatience, "all the harm in the world. You'll allow me to understand my own business. It is clearly time for a man to interfere. I shall see Mr. Ridsdale to-morrow, if all the women in the world were to try their skill and hold me back. Hold your tongue, Mrs. Despard; be quiet, Lottie. When a man is a husband and a father he is the best judge of his own duties. It is now my time to interfere."

Polly was really concerned; she had a fellow feeling for the girl whose rights were thus interfered with. "Don't you mind," she said, turning to Lottie with a half-audible whisper. "If he's coming to the point himself it won't do no harm, and if he ain't it will give him a push, and let him see what's expected of him. I ain't one for interfering myself, but if you can't help it you must just put up with it; and I don't think, after all, it will do so very much harm."

Now Lottie ought to have been grateful for this well-intentioned and amiable remark, but she was not. On the contrary, her anger rose more wildly against the stranger who thus attempted to console her, than it did against her father, whose sudden resolution was so painful to her. She gave Polly a look of wrath, and, forgetting even civility, darted out of the room and upstairs in vehement resentment. Polly was not so much angry as amazed to the point of consternation. She gasped for the breath which was taken away by Lottie's sudden flight. "Well!" she exclaimed, "that's manners, that is! that's what you call being brought up careful! A young unmarried girl, as is nothing and nobody, rushing out of a room like that before a married lady and her Pa's wife!"

Lottie, however, was in a passion of alarm, which drove everything else out of her head. Of all things that seemed to her most to be avoided, a meeting between her father and Rollo at this crisis was the worst. She left her room no more that evening, but sat and pondered what she could do to avert the danger. True, without a meeting between them it would be impossible that her love should have its legitimate sanction, and that the beginning of her new life should be honest and straightforward, as it ought. But partly because she had schooled herself to think (by way of excusing Rollo's silence) that a meeting between him and her father would only make him less respectful of the Captain's pretensions and the "family" which Lottie still with forlorn faith believed in, and partly because the visit of a father to ask a lover's "intentions" was perhaps the very last way in which a beginning of intercourse could be agreeably established, it seemed to Lottie that she would do anything in the world to prevent this meeting. With this view she wrote one little note and then another to warn Rollo—writing with cold fingers but a beating heart, hot with anxiety and trouble, upon the corner of her little dressing-table—for there was no room for any other convenience of a table in the small, old-fashioned chamber. But when she had at last achieved a composition of one which seemed to express feebly yet sufficiently what she wanted to say, the question arose, How was it to get to Rollo? She had no one to send. She dared not trust it to Law, for that would involve an explanation, and there was no one else at Lottie's command. A thought of Captain Temple floated across her mind; but how could she employ him upon such an errand, which would involve a still more difficult explanation? At last she burnt regretfully by the flame of her candle the very last of these effusions, and decided that she must trust to the chances of the morrow. She had promised to be at the elm-tree in the morning to bid Rollo good-by. She must manage, then, to get him to go away before matins were over and her father free. But it was with an anxious heart that Lottie, when her candle burned out, crept cold and troubled to bed, chilled to the bone, yet with a brow which burned and throbbed with excitement. Law did not come in till after she had fallen asleep. Law, whom she had watched over so anxiously, was, at this crisis of Lottie's personal history and his own, left entirely to himself.

In the morning she managed to run out immediately after breakfast, just as the air began to vibrate with the Abbey bells, and, after some anxious waiting under the elm, at last, to her great relief, saw Rollo coming. Lottie was not able to disguise her anxiety or her desire for his departure. "Never mind speaking to me," she said. "Do not waste time. Oh, Rollo, forgive me—no, it is not to get rid of you," she cried, and then she told him the incident of last night.

Rollo's eyes gave forth a gleam of disgust when he heard of the chance of being stopped by Captain Despard to enquire his "intentions." He laughed, and Lottie thought instinctively that this was a sound of merriment which she would never wish to hear again. But his face brightened as he turned to Lottie, who was so anxious to save him from this ordeal. "My faithful Lottie!" he said, pressing her close to him. There was nobody stirring in the winterly morning; but yet day requires more reserve than the early darkness of night.

"But go, go, Rollo. I want you to be gone before they are out of the Abbey," she cried, breathless.

"My dear love—my only love," he said, holding both her hands in his.

"Oh, Rollo, is it not only for a day or two? You are so serious, you frighten me—but go, go, that you may not meet anyone," she said.

"Yes, it is only for a day or two, my darling," he replied. "On Friday, my Lottie, at five under this tree. You won't fail me?"

"Never," she said, with her blue eyes full of sweet tears. And then they kissed in the eye of day, all the silent world looking on.

"No," he said, with fervour—"never; you will never fail me; you will always be true."

And so they parted, she watching jealously while he took his way, not by the common road, but down the windings of the Slopes, that he might be safe, that no one might annoy him. "Till Friday!" he called to her in the silence, waving his hand as he turned the corner out of her sight. She drew a long breath of relief when she saw him emerge alone farther down upon the road that led to the railway. The Signor was only then beginning the voluntary, and Captain Despard evidently could not ask Rollo Ridsdale his "intentions" that day. Lottie waved her hand to her lover, though he was too far off to see her, and said to herself, "Till Friday," with a sudden realisation all of these words implied—another life, a new heaven and a new earth; love, and tenderness, and worship instead of the careless use and wont of the family; to be first instead of last; to be happy and at rest instead of tormented at everybody's caprice; to be with Rollo, who loved her, always, for ever and ever, with no more risk of losing him or being forgotten. Her heart overflowed with sweetness, her eyes with soft tears of joy. Out of that enchanted land she went back for a little while into common life, but not in any common way. The sunshine, which had been slow to shine, broke out over the Dean's Walk as she emerged from under the shadow of the trees; the path was cleared for her; the music pealed out from the Abbey. Unconsciously her steps fell into a kind of stately movement, keeping time. In her blessedness she moved softly on towards the shadow of the house in which she had now but a few days to live—like a princess walking to her coronation, like a martyr to her agony. Who could tell in which of the two the best similitude lay?

CHAPTER XL
THE EFFECT OF GOOD FORTUNE: LAW

Law had left Mr. Ashford, not knowing, as the vulgar have it, if he stood on his head or his heels. He had somewhat despised the Minor Canon, not only as a clergyman and an instructor, intending to put something into Law's luckless brains, yet without force enough to do it effectually, but as a man, much too mild and gentle to make any head against the deceitfulness of mankind, and all those guiles and pretences in which an unwilling student like Law knows himself so much more profoundly informed than any of his pastors and teachers can be. The sense of superiority with which such a youth, learned in all manner of "dodges" and devices for eluding work, contemplates the innocent senior who has faith in his excuses, was strong in Law's mind towards his last tutor, who was so much less knowing than any of the others, that he had taken him "for nothing," without even the pay which his earlier instructor, Mr. Langton, had been supposed to receive: supposed—for Captain Despard was paymaster, and he was not any more to be trusted to for recollecting quarter-day than Law was to be trusted to for doing his work. But Mr. Ashford had never said anything about pay. He had taken Law for his sister's sake, "for love," as the young man said lightly; taken him as an experiment, to see what could be made of him, and kept him on without a word on either side of remuneration. This curious conduct, which might have made the pupil grateful, had no such result, but filled him instead with a more entire contempt for the intellects of his benefactor. It is easy, in the estimation of young men like Law, to be learned and wise in book-learning, yet a "stupid" in life; and if anything could have made this fact more clear, it would have been the irregularity of the business transaction as between a non-paying pupil and a "coach" who gave just as much attention to him as if he had been an important source of revenue. "What a soft he must be! What a stupid he is," had been Law's standing reflection. But he had liked all the same the object of his scorn, and had felt "old Ashford" to be "very jolly," notwithstanding his foolish believingness, and still more foolish indifference to his own profit. It was this which had made him go to the Minor Canon with such a frankness of appeal—but he had not been in the least prepared for the reply he received. It took away his breath. Though it was a superlative proof of the same "softness" which had made Mr. Ashford receive a pupil who paid him nothing, the dazzled youth could no longer regard it with contempt. Though he was tolerably fortified against invasions of emotion, there was something in this which penetrated to his heart. Suddenly, in a moment, to be lifted out of his dull struggle with books which he could not understand, and hopeless anticipation of an ordeal he could never pass, and to have the desire of his heart given to him, without any trouble of his, without price or reward, was all very wonderful to Law. At first he could not believe it. To think "old Ashford" was joking—to think that a man so impractical did not put the ordinary meaning into his words—this was the first natural explanation; but when the Minor Canon's first recollection that "he knew a man" brightened into the prospect of money to pay the young emigrant's passage, and an actual beginning of his career, Law did not know, as we have said, whether he was standing upon solid ground or floating in the air. The happiness was almost too much for him. He went up to London next day by Mr. Ashford's suggestion, and, at his cost, to learn all particulars about the voyage, but kept his own secret until it had gained so much of solid foundation as the actual sight of a ship which was bound for Australia, a printed account of the times of sailing, and fares, and an outfitter's list of indispensables, could give; then, still dazzled by the sudden fulfilment of his wishes, but feeling his own importance, and the seriousness of his position as a future emigrant, Law had endeavoured to find an opportunity of communicating the great news to Lottie, but had failed, as has been seen. And having thus failed, and seeing in her none of the eager desire to know what he was about, which he thought would have been natural in circumstances so profoundly interesting, Law got up from the table and went out with a certain sense of injury in his mind. He saw there was "something up" in respect to his sister herself, but he did not take very much interest in that. Yet he thought it curiously selfish of her, almost incomprehensibly selfish, to ask no question, show no concern in what was happening to him. He had said, "I am going to Australia!" but had he said, "I am going to play football," she could not have taken it more calmly; and she had never asked a question since. What funny creatures women are, one time so anxious about you, another time caring nothing, Law said to himself; but he was not at all conscious that it might have been natural for him too to take some interest in Lottie's affairs. He did not. It was some rubbish, he supposed, about that fellow Ridsdale. He thought of the whole business with contempt. Far more important, beyond all comparison, were those affairs which were his own.

And when he went out, a little angry, irritated, but full of excitement and elation, and eager to find somebody who would take due interest in the story of his good fortune, where could Law's footsteps stray but to the place where they had turned so often in his idleness and hopelessness? He had gone once before since the visit of Polly, and had been confronted by Mrs. Welting, now established in the workroom, to the confusion of all the little schemes of amusement by which the girls had solaced the tedium of their lives. "Mother" had been glad enough to be allowed to look after her house in quiet, and the rest of the family, without troubling herself about her girls. But the sharp prick of Polly's denunciation had given Mrs. Welting new ideas of her duty. Would she let it be said by an artful creature like that, who had done the same thing herself, as *her* daughters were laying themselves out to catch a gentleman? Not for all the world! She would not have a girl of hers marry a gentleman, not for anything, Mrs. Welting said. She forbade the little expeditions they were in the habit of making in turns for thread and buttons. She would not allow even the *Family Herald*. She scolded "for nothing at all," resenting her compulsory attendance there, and banishment from her domestic concerns. The workroom was quite changed. There was no jollity in it, no visitors, not half so much chatter as had been carried on gaily while Polly was paramount. "She took all the good herself, but she never could bear seeing anyone else happy," Emma said, who was doubly aggrieved. And it could not be said that the work improved under this discipline. The moment altogether was not happy; and when Law, by dint of wandering about the windows, and whistling various airs known to the workroom, made his presence known, Emma, when her mother withdrew, as she did perforce as the evening got on, and it became necessary to look after the family supper, the younger children, and her lodgers—came cautiously out to meet him, with a cloak about her shoulders. "I haven't got a moment to stay," Emma said. "Mother would take off my head if she found me out!" Yet she suffered herself to be drawn a few steps from the door, and round the corner to the riverside, where, on this wintry evening, there was nobody about, and the river itself in the darkness was only discernible by the white swell and foam round the piers of the bridge, by which it rushed on its headlong passage to the weir. Here, now going, now coming, a few wary steps at a time, awaiting a possible warning from the window of the lighted workroom, the two wandered in the damp darkness, and Emma, opening large eyes of astonishment, heard of all that was about to happen. "Old Ashford has behaved like a brick," Law said. "He is going to give me introductions to people he knows, and he means to give me my passage-money too, and something to begin upon!"

"Lor!" cried Emma, "what is it for? Is he going to marry your sister?" Her attention was awakened, but she did not think she had anything to do with it; she was so much afraid of not hearing any possible tap on the window, or not having time to run home before her absence was discovered.

"Now look here, Emma," said Law. He did not speak with any enthusiasm of tenderness, but calmly, as having something serious to propose. "If I go away, you know, it's for life; it's not gone to-day and back to-morrow, like a soldier ordered off to the Colonies. I'm going to make my living, and my fortune, if I can, and settle there for life. No, nobody's knocking at the window. Can't you give me your attention for a moment? I tell you, if I go, it's for life."

"Lor!" said Emma, startled. "You don't mean to say as you've come to say good-bye, Mr. Law? and you as always said you were so true. But I do believe none of you young men ever remembers nor thinks what he's been saying," she added with a half whimper. A lover's desertion is never a pleasant thing in any condition of life.

"It's just because of that I'm here," said Law, sturdily. "I remember all I've ever said. I've come to put it to you, Emma, straightforward. I am going away, as I tell you, for life. Will you come with me? that's the question. There is not very much to spare, and there's the outfit to get, but it will go hard if I can't draw old Ashford for your passage-money," said the grateful recipient of the Minor Canon's bounty; "and it would be a new start and a new life, and I'd do the best I could for you. Emma, you must make up your mind quick, for there isn't much time. The boat sails—well, I can't exactly tell you when she sails; but in a fortnight or so—"

"A fortnight!" Emma cried, with a sense of dismay.

"Yes. We needn't have a very grand wedding, need we? Emigrants must be careful both of their money and their time."

"Emigrants? I don't know what you mean by emigrants—it don't sound much," said the girl, with a cloud upon her face.

"No, it is not very fine. It means people that are going to settle far away, on the other side of the world. Australia is—I don't know how many thousand miles away."

"Can you go there by land?" said Emma. "You needn't laugh—how was I to know? Oh, I can't abide going in a ship."

"That's a pity, for you can't go in anything else. But it's a fine big ship, and every care taken. Look here, Emma, you must make up your mind. Will you go?"

"Oh, I don't know," cried Emma; "I can't tell; how long would you be in the ship? It isn't what I ever expected," she said in a plaintive voice. "A hurry, and a fuss, and then a long sea-voyage. Oh, I don't think I should like it, Mr. Law."

"The question is, do you like me?" said Law, with a little thrill in his deep yet boyish bass. "You couldn't like the parting and all that—it wouldn't be natural; but do you like *me* well enough to put up with it? I don't want you to do anything you don't like, but when I go it will be for good, and you must just make up your mind which you like best—to go with me, though there's a good deal of trouble, or to stay at home, and good-bye to me for ever."

At this, Emma began to cry. "Oh, I shouldn't like to say good-bye for ever," she said; "I always hated saying good-bye. I don't know what to do; it would be good-bye to mother, and Ellen, and them all. And never to come back again would be awful! I shouldn't mind if it was for a year or two years, but never to come back—I don't know what to do."

"We might come home on a visit, if we got very rich," said Law, "or we might have some of the others out to see us."

"Oh, for a visit!" said Emma. "But they'd miss me dreadful in the workroom. Oh, I wish I knew what to say."

"You must choose for yourself—you must please yourself," said Law, a little piqued by the girl's many doubts; then he softened again. "You know, Emma," he said, "when a girl gets married it's very seldom she has her own people near her, and I don't know that it's a good thing when she has. People say, at least, husband and wife ought to be enough for each other. And, supposing it was only to London, it would still be away from them."

"Oh, but it would be different," cried Emma; "if one could come back now and again, and see them all; but to live always hundreds of thousands of miles away."

"Not hundreds of thousands; but a long voyage that takes months—"

"Months!" Emma uttered a cry. "Too far to have mother if you were ill," she said, casting her mind over the eventualities of the future; "too far, a deal too far for a trip to see one. I don't think it would be nice at all. Mr. Law, couldn't you, oh, couldn't you stop at home?"

"Perhaps you'd tell me what I should do if I stayed at home," said Law, not without a touch of contempt. "It's more than I can tell. No, I can't stay at home. There is nothing I could do here. It is Australia or nothing, Emma; you must make up your mind to that."

"Oh, but I don't see why you shouldn't stay in London; there are always places to be got there; you might look in the papers and see. Mother used to get the *Times* from the public-house, a penny an hour, when Willie was out of a place. Did you ever answer any advertisement, or try—really try?"

"All that is nothing to the purpose," said Law, with some impatience. "The advertisements may be all very well, but I know nothing about them. I am going to Australia whether or not. I've quite made up my mind. Now the thing is, will you come too?"

Emma did not know what answer to make. The going away was appalling, but to lose her gentleman-lover, though he was banished from the workroom, was a great humiliation. Then she could not but feel that there was a certain excitement and importance in the idea of preparing for a sudden voyage, and being married at seventeen, the first of the family. But when she thought of the sea and the ship, and the separation from everything, Emma's strength of mind gave way. She could not do that. The end was that, driven back and forward between the two, she at last faltered forth a desire to consult "Mother" before deciding. Law, though he was contemptuous of this weakness, yet could not say anything against it. Perhaps it was necessary that a girl should own such a subjection. "If you do, I can tell you beforehand what she will say," he cried. "Then Ellen; I'll ask Ellen," said Emma. "Oh, I can't settle it out of my own head." And then the girl started, hearing the signal on the window, and fled from him, breathless. "Mother's come to shut up," she said. Law walked away, not without satisfaction, when this end had been attained. He was more anxious to have the question settled than he was anxious to have Emma. Indeed, he was not at all blind to the fact that he was too young to marry, and that there were disadvantages in hampering himself even in Australia with such a permanent companion. Then, too, all that he could hope for from Mr. Ashford was enough for his own outfit and passage, and he did not see how hers was to be managed. But, still, Law had been "keeping company" with Emma for some time, and he acknowledged the duties of that condition according to the interpretation put upon it in the order to which Emma belonged. Clearly, when good fortune came to a young man who was keeping company with a young woman, it was right that he should offer her a share of it. If she did not accept it, so much the better; he would have done what honour required without any further trouble. As Law walked up the hill again, he reflected that on the whole it would be much better if he were allowed to go to Australia alone. No one could know how things would turn out. Perhaps the man Mr. Ashford knew might be of little use, perhaps he might have to go from one place to another; or he might not succeed at first; or many things might happen which would make a wife an undesirable burden. He could not but hope that things might so arrange themselves as that Emma should drop back into her natural sphere in the workroom, and he be left free. Poor little Emma! if this were the case, he would buy her a locket as a keepsake off Mr. Ashford's money, and take leave of her with comfort. But in the other case, if she should make up her mind to go with him, Law was ready to accept the alternative. His good fortune put him doubly on his honour. He would prefer to be free, yet, if he were held to it, he was prepared to do his duty. He would not let her perceive that he did not want her. But, on the whole, he would be much better satisfied if "Mother" interfered. Having disposed of this matter, Law began to think of his outfit, which was very important, wondering, by the way, if Emma went, whether her family would provide hers? but yet keeping this question, as uncertain, quite in the background. He recalled to himself the list he had got in his pocket, with its dozens of shirts and socks, with no small satisfaction. Was it possible that he could become the owner of all that? The thought of becoming the owner of a wife he took calmly, hoping he might still avoid the necessity; but to have such a wardrobe was exciting and delightful. He determined to get Lottie to show him how to mend a hole and sew on a button. To think that Lottie knew nothing about his plans, and had never asked him what he meant, bewildered him when he thought of it. What could be "up" in respect to her? Something like anxiety crossed Law's mind; at least, it was something as much like anxiety as he was capable of—a mingling of surprise and indignation; for were not his affairs a great deal more important than anything affecting herself could be? This was the idea of both. Law was going to Australia, but Lottie was going to be married, a still more important event! and each felt that in heaven and earth no other such absorbing interest existed. It must be said, however, for Lottie, that Law's whispered communication counted for nothing with her, since she knew no way in which it could be possible. Wild hopes that came to nothing had gleamed across his firmament before. How could he go to Australia? As easy to say that he was going to the moon; and in this way it took no hold upon her mind; while he, for his part, had no clue whatever to the disturbing influence in Lottie's thoughts.

CHAPTER XLI THE EFFECT OF GOOD FORTUNE: ROLLO

The night after that decisive talk upon the Slopes was a trying one for Rollo Ridsdale. He went home with the fumes of his resolution in his mind. Now the die was cast. Whatever prudence might say against it, the decision was made, and his life settled for him, partly by circumstances, but much more by his personal will and deed. And he did not regret what he had done. It was a tremendous risk to run; but he had confidence that Lottie's voice was as good as a fortune, and that in the long run there would be nothing really imprudent in it. Of course it must be kept entirely "quiet." No indiscreet announcements in the newspapers, no unnecessary publicity must be given to the marriage. Whosoever was absolutely concerned should know; but for the general public, what did it matter to them whether the bond which bound a man of fashion to a celebrated singer was legitimate or not? Lottie would not wish for society, she would not feel the want of society, and particularly in the interval, while she was still not a celebrated singer, it was specially necessary that all should be kept "quiet." He would take her to Italy, and it would be not at all needful to introduce any stray acquaintance who might happen to turn up, to his wife. In short, there was no occasion for introducing anyone to her. Lottie would not want anything. She would be content with himself. Poor darling! what wonderful trust there was in her! By this time he was able to half-laugh at his own guilty intention, which she had so completely extinguished by her inability to understand it, her perfect acceptance of it as all that was honourable and tender. He was going to do the right thing now—certainly the right thing, without any mistake about it; but still that it should be made to look like the wrong thing, was the idea in Rollo's mind. He would take her to Italy and train her for her future career; but neither at the present time nor in the future would it be necessary to put the dots upon the i's in respect to her position. As for Lottie, he knew very well that she, having no doubt about her position, would not insist upon any publication of it. It would never once occur to her that there was any possibility of being misconstrued.

With these thoughts in his mind, Rollo dressed very hastily for dinner, as he had lingered with Lottie to the last moment. And as it happened, this was the very evening which Augusta chose for discussing openly the subject to which she had, without speaking of it, already devoted all her powers of research since she had arrived at home. In the evening after dinner Rollo was the only one of the gentlemen who came into the drawing-room. Augusta's husband was an inoffensive and silent man, with what are called "refined tastes." For one thing he was in a mild way an antiquary. He did not enter very much into his wife's life, nor she into his. She was fashionable, he had refined tastes; they were perfectly good friends; and though not yet married six months, followed each their own way. Spencer Daventry had gone to his father-in-law's study accordingly, to investigate some rare books, and his wife was in the drawing-room alone—that is, not exactly alone, for Lady Caroline was "on the sofa." When Lady Caroline was on the sofa she did not trouble anybody much, and even the coming in of the lamps had not disturbed her. She had "just closed her eyes." Her dress was carefully drawn over her feet by Mrs. Daventry's care, and a wadded *couvre-pied* in crimson satin laid over them. Augusta liked to see to every little decorum, and would have thought the toe of her mother's innocent shoe an improper revelation. Perhaps it was by her orders that Mr. Daventry had not come in. There was no company that evening, and when Rollo entered the drawing-room, he saw at once that he had fallen into a trap. Augusta sat on a comfortable chair by the fire, with a small table near her and a lamp upon it. The other lights were far away, candles twinkling in the distance on the piano, and here and there against the walls: but only this one spot by the fire in warm and full light; and a vacant chair stood invitingly on the other side of Augusta's table. No more snug arrangement for a *tête-à-tête* could have been, for Lady Caroline was nothing but a bit of still life—more still almost than the rest of the furniture. Augusta looked up as her cousin came in, with a smile.

"Alone?" she said; "then come here, Rollo, and let us have a talk."

Rollo would not have been Rollo if he had felt any repugnance to this amusement. Needless to say that in their boy and girl days there had been passages of something they were pleased to call love between the cousins; and equally needless to add that all this had long been over, both being far too sensible (though one had been led astray by Lottie, to his own consternation and confusion) to think of any serious conclusion to such a youthful folly. Rollo sat down with mingled pleasure and alarm. He liked a confidential talk with any woman; but in this case he was not without fear.

And his fears were thoroughly well founded as it turned out. After a few preliminaries about nothing at all, Augusta suddenly plunged into her subject.

"I am very glad," she said, "to have a chance of speaking to you, by ourselves. Mamma does not pay any attention; it is quite the same as if she

were not there. You know I've always taken a great interest in you, Rollo. We are cousins, and we are very old friends—more like brother and sister."

"I demur to the brother and sister; but as old friends as memory can go," said he; "and very happy to be permitted all the privileges of a cousin—with such a good fellow as Daventry added on."

"Oh, yes. Spencer's very nice," said she. "He takes very kindly to my people; but it is not about Spencer I want to talk to you, Rollo, but about yourself."

"That's so much the better," said Rollo; "for I might not have liked bridal raptures, not being able, you know, Augusta, quite to forget—"

"Oh, that's all nonsense," said Augusta, with the faintest of blushes; "bridal fiddlesticks! People in the world keep clear of all that nonsense, heaven be praised. No, Rollo, it's about yourself. I am very anxious about you."

"Angelic cousin!—but there is no cause for anxiety that I know of in me."

"Oh, yes, Rollo, there is great cause of anxiety. I must speak to you quite frankly. When I was married you had never seen Lottie Despard—"

"Miss Despard!" He repeated the name in a surprised tone and with eyes full of astonishment. He was glad of the opportunity of looking to the buckles of his armour and preparing for the onset; and therefore he made the surprise of the exclamation as telling as he could. "What can she have to do with your anxiety?" he said.

"Yes, Lottie Despard. Oh, she has a great deal to do with it. Rollo, how can you think that any good can come of such a flirtation either to you or the girl?"

"Flirtation, Augusta?"

"Yes, flirtation, or something worse. Why do you always go to her lessons? Oh, I know you always go. She can't sing a bit, poor thing; and it only fills her poor heart with vanity and nonsense; and you meet her when you walk out. Don't contradict me, please. Should I say so, if I had not made quite sure? I know the view you men take of honour. You think when a girl is concerned you are bound to deny everything. So you may be sure I did not say it till I had made quite sure. Now, Rollo, I ask you what can possibly come of anything of this kind? Of course you only mean to amuse yourself; and of course it is the girl's fault if she gets herself talked about; for she must know as well as I do that there can be nothing in it; but for all that—"

"You take away my breath," said Rollo; "you seem to know so much better than I do the things that have happened or are happening to myself."

"I do," said Augusta, "for I have been thinking about it, and you have not. You have just done what was pleasant at the moment, and never taken any thought. You are doing a great deal of harm to Lottie, poor thing, filling her head with silly fancies, and turning her against people of her own class. And suppose some really *nice* girl were to turn up, some one with money, what would she think of you, dangling for ever after a young woman who is not even in society? I am taking it for granted that it is only a silly flirtation: for as for anything worse," said Augusta, with severity, "it cannot be supposed for a moment that *I* could speak to you of that; but you know very well, Rollo, a man of the world, like you, how very dreadful, how fatal all those sort of entanglements are, even when you don't look at them from a high moral point of view."

"You make me out a pretty character," said Rollo, with an angry smile. "I never knew I was a Lovelace till now."

"Oh, all you men are the same," said Augusta, "if women will let you. Women have themselves to thank when anything happens, for it is of ten times more importance to them than it is to you. A man is none the worse for things that would ruin a girl for ever. But, still, you are not in a position to be careless of what people say. You have not a penny, Rollo; and I don't believe in your opera. The only way in which you will ever have anything is by a suitable marriage. Suppose that any of your relations were to find a really nice person for you, and you were to spoil it all by a folly like this! That is how I look at it. To ruin yourself for a girl's pretty face! and her voice—when she can't sing a note!"

"Am I to infer that you have got a nice person for me?" said Rollo, furious inwardly, yet keeping his temper, and turning the conversation in this direction by way of diverting it from more dangerous subjects. And then Augusta (drawing somewhat upon her imagination, it must be allowed) told him of a very nice person indeed. Rollo listened, by way of securing his escape; but by and by he got slightly interested, in spite of himself. This really nice girl was coming to the Deanery for two or three days. She had a hundred thousand pounds. She had heard of Rollo Ridsdale, and already "took an interest" in him. It was perhaps partly fiction, for the visit of this golden girl to the Deanery was not by any means settled—but yet there was in it a germ of fact. "It is an opportunity that never may occur again," Augusta said, like a shop that is selling off. And indeed it was a sale which she would have greatly liked to negotiate, though Rollo was less the buyer than the piece of goods of which sale was to be made.

A hundred thousand pounds! He could not help thinking of it later in the evening, when he smoked his cigar, and as he went to bed. His affairs seemed to him to be managed by some malign and tricky spirit. Just at this moment, when he was pledged to the most imprudent marriage that could be conceived, was it not just his luck that fate should take the opportunity of dangling such a prize before him? A hundred thousand pounds! Why was it not Lottie that had this money? or why, as she had no money, had she been thrown in his way? To be sure she had a voice, which was as good as a fortune, but not equal to a hundred thousand pounds. However, he said to himself, there was no help for it now. All this happened before the brief interview on the hill, which sent him off to town before the hour he intended, and which proved to him, over and over again, her trust in him, which was beyond anything he had ever dreamed of. That she should guard him even from her father, that she should believe in him, to the disdain of every safeguard which the vulgar mind relied on, astonished, confounded, and impressed his mind beyond description. To deceive her would be the easiest thing in the world, but, at the same time, would it not be the most impossible thing, the last that any man not a villain could do? And there was besides a glimmering perception in Rollo's mind that deception would only be practicable up to a certain point, and that the scorn and horror and indignation with which Lottie would turn upon the criminal who had intended shame to her, would be something as much unlike the ordinary rage of a wronged woman as her trust was beyond the ordinary suspicious smoothness of ordinary belief. Shame and she had nothing to do with each other. She might die in the agony of the discovery, but first her eyes, her lips, the passion of her indignant purity would slay. With a deep regret he thought of the easier tie. Augusta's words had been those of a silly woman when she spoke of fatal entanglements. On the contrary, marriage was the fatal thing. The other—what harm would it have done? None to Lottie in her career; no one would have thought any the worse of her. People would be sure to suppose that something of the kind had occurred in a singer's life, whether it was true or not. It would have done her no harm; and it would not have done Rollo any harm. To think of it as fatal was the greatest folly. On the contrary, they would have been of use to each other now, and after they would each have been free to consult their own interests. He could not help thinking very regretfully of this so easy, agreeable expedient, which would have been anything but fatal. To be sure, this was not, as Augusta said, a high moral point of view; but Rollo did not pretend to be a moralist. All these thoughts poured through his mind again as he went to London, with the full intention of getting a license for his marriage, and making all the arrangements which would bind Lottie to him as his wife. He was obliged to do this; he could not help himself. Much rather would he have done anything else—taken the other alternative—but it was not possible. There was but this one thing to do—a thing which put it entirely out of his power for ever and ever to consider the claims of any really nice person with a hundred thousand pounds at her disposal. Rollo did not pretend to himself that he took the decisive step with any satisfaction. He was no triumphant bridegroom; but he was a true lover, and not a villain, and regretfully but steadfastly he gave himself up to what he had to do.

It was too late to do anything in respect to the license when he arrived in town, but there were many other things to be settled, in order to make a considerably long absence practicable, and these he arranged in his own mind as he approached his journey's end. For one thing, he had the funds to provide; and that, as will be readily perceived, was no small matter. He walked out of the railway station, pondering this in his mind. It was a grave question, not one to be lightly solved. He did not want to return to town till the season should have begun. No doubt five months' honeymooning would bore any man, but he felt it to be too important to think of mere personal amusement; and he could always make expeditions himself to more lively places, and get a share of any amusement that might be going, when he had settled down Lottie to her studies, under the best masters that were to be had. All this was quite easily settled; but for an absence of five months, if you have not any income to speak of, it is necessary to have an understanding with your bankers, or somebody else. He meant to try his bankers, for his confidence in Lottie's future success was extreme, and he felt justified in speaking of it as money which his future wife would be entitled to. All these plans he was laying very deliberately in his head, calculating how much he would need, and various other particulars, when the face of a man approaching in a hansom suddenly struck him. It was Rixon, his father's confidential servant, a man who had been in Lord Courtland's service as long as anybody could recollect. What was he doing there? The hansom was directing its course towards the railway from which Rollo had just come, and Rixon's countenance was of an extreme gravity. What could it mean? Could anything have happened? Rollo saw the hansom pass, but its occupant did not see him. He could not banish from his thoughts the idea that something must have happened—that it was to tell him something, some news more or less terrible that Rixon was on his way to the railway which went to St. Michael's. After a moment's hesitation he turned and went back to the station, not being able to divest himself of this idea. To be sure Rixon might be going somewhere on business of his own; he might be looking grave about his own affairs. Still Rollo turned and went back; in any case it was best to know. The man was standing among several others, waiting to take his ticket for the train, when Rollo re-entered the station; he was getting his money out of his pocket to pay his fare; but looking up as he did this, Rixon started, put his money back, and immediately disengaged himself from the *queue*. It was then a message from home of sufficient importance to be sent by special envoy. Rollo had time to examine this bearer of ill-news as he approached. What but ill-news was ever so urgent? special messengers do not travel about to stray sons of a family with news of birth or bridal. There is but one thing which calls for such state, and that is death. Rollo ran over all the chances in a moment, in his mind. His father—if it were his father there would be a little delay, a little ready money, more need than ever, and a very good excuse, for keeping everything quiet. It was not absolute want of feeling that suggested this thought. If it was his father there would be many reasons for being sorry. Home, with your brother at the head of affairs, is not home like your father's house. And Lord Courtland, though his second son had worn out his kindness, was still kind more or less. Rollo was not insensible; he felt the dull consciousness of a blow before he received it, as he fixed his eyes upon Rixon's mournful countenance, and the band on his hat.

"What is the matter?" he said, as the man approached. "What has happened? You were going to me? Tell me at once what it is."

"I beg your pardon, Sir," said Rixon, with the perpetual apology of a well-bred servant. "Yes, Sir, I was going to St. Michael's. My lord sent me to tell you—"

"Thank heaven, that it is not my father! You mean that my father sent you? That is a relief," said Rollo, drawing a long breath.

"Yes, my—Sir!" said Rixon, with confusion, "My lord is in the enjoyment of perfect health—at least as good as is compatible with the great misfortune, the catastrophe that has—snatched—"

"What do you mean?" said Rollo. Rixon was fond of long words. He laughed, "You are always mysterious. But if my father is all right—"

"Oh, don't! my—don't, Sir!" said the man, "laughing is not what ought to be on your lips at such a moment. Your brother has had an accident—"

"My brother—Ridsdale? Good heavens! Can't you speak out? What has happened?" said Rollo, with blanched cheeks. Horror, fear, hope, all sprung up within him, indistinguishable the one from the other. The moment seemed a year during which he stood waiting for Rixon's next words.

"It is too true, my lord," said the man, and the address threw around Rollo a sudden gleam of growing light. "Your brother had a terrible accident on the hunting-field. His horse stumbled on King's Mead, at that bad fence by Willowbrook. He was taken up insensible, and died before he could be got home. Things are in a terrible state at Courtlands. I was sent to let your lordship know. My lord would be glad if you would come home at once."

Rollo staggered back, and put himself against the wall. A cold moisture burst out over him. He grew so pale that Rixon thought he was going to faint. The man said afterwards that he could not have believed that Mr. Ridsdale had so much feeling. And partly it was feeling as Rixon thought. For the first moment the thought that his brother, upon whom fate had always smiled—Ridsdale! *Ridsdale!*—the very impersonation of prosperity and good fortune, should be lying dead, actually dead, at his age, with all his prospects, appalled him. It seemed too much, unnatural, beyond all possibility of belief. Then the blood rushed back through all his veins with a flush and suffusion of sudden heat. The change alarmed the messenger of so much evil and so much good. He put out his hand to support his young master. "My lord, my lord!" he said (they were words which Rixon loved to repeat, and which added to his own dignity as a gentleman's gentleman), "remember your father; now that your lamented brother is gone, all his lordship's trust is in you."

Rollo waved his hand, not caring for the moment to speak. "Let me alone!" he said. "Let me alone! leave me to myself." And it did not take him long to recover and shake off the horrible impression, and realise the astounding change that had occurred. Perhaps it is not possible that the death of a brother, which produces so extraordinary and beneficial a change in the situation and prospects of the next in succession, can be regarded with the natural feeling which such an event uncomplicated by loss or gain of a pecuniary kind calls forth. There was a sudden shock, then a consciousness that something was expected from him, some show of grief and profound distress; and then a bewildering, overwhelming, stupefying, yet exciting realisation of the change thus suddenly accomplished in himself. He was no longer merely Rollo, a fashionable adventurer, dealing in every kind of doubtful speculation, and legitimatised gambling, a man of no importance to anyone, and free to carry out whatever schemes might come into his head; but now—an altogether different person—Lord Ridsdale, his father's heir; the future head of a great family; a future peer; and already endowed with all the importance of an heir-apparent. The world seemed to go round and round with Rollo, and when it settled again out of the whirling and pale confusion as of an earthquake, it was not any longer the same world. The proportion of things had changed in the twinkling of an eye. The distant and the near had changed places. What was close to him before receded; what was far away became near. In the hurry of his thoughts he could not even think. Pain mingled with everything, with the giddiness of a strange elation, with the bewilderment of a surprise more startling than any that had ever come to him before in all his life. Ridsdale!—he who had always been so smiling and prosperous; he to whom everything was forgiven; whose sins were only peccadilloes; whose lightest schoolboy successes were trumpeted abroad, whose movements were recorded where-ever he went; it was inconceivable that he should be lying—dead; inconceivable that Rollo, the detrimental, the one in the family whom all disapproved of, should be put in his place, and succeed to all his privileges and exemptions. It did not seem possible. It needed Rixon saying my lord to him at every moment, to make the curious fiction seem true. Rixon got a cab to drive his young master to the other station, by which he must go to Courtlands; and Rollo—

leaving all his former life behind him, leaving his license, his marriage, his bride, in the opposite direction, fading into misty spectres—turned his back upon all that had been most important to him half an hour ago, and drove away.

He went through that day like a dream—the whole course of his existence turned into another channel. He got home, rolling up to the familiar door with sensations so different from any that had ever moved him when entering that door before. He looked at it this time with a feeling of proprietorship. It had been his home for all his early life; but now it was going to be *his own*, which is very different. He looked at the very trees with a different feeling, wondering why so many should be marked for cutting down. What had they been doing to want to get rid of so many trees? When he went into the room where his brother lay dead, it was to him as if a waxen image lay there, as if it were all a skilful scene, arranged to make believe that such a change, one man substituted for another, could be *real*. To Rollo it did not seem to be real. It was the younger son who had died, with all his busy schemes—his plans for the future, his contrivances to get money, and the strange connections which he had formed. Rollo, who was the founder of the new opera, the partner of the bustling manager; it was he who was lying on that bed. All his plans would be buried with him—his Bohemianism, his enterprises, his—. What was it that the poor fool had gone in for, the last of all his undertakings, the thing in which he had been happily arrested ere he could harm himself or embarrass the family?—his love—. It was when standing by the bed on which his brother lay dead that this thought suddenly darted into the new Lord Ridsdale's mind. He turned away with a half groan. Providence had interposed to prevent that foolish fellow from consummating his fate. He had not yet reached the highest pitch of folly when the blow fell. Something there was which the family had escaped. When the key was turned again in the door, and he went back to another darkened room and heard all about the accident, it was almost on his lips to contradict the speakers, and tell them it was not Ridsdale that was dead. But he did not do so. He preserved his decorum and seriousness. He was "very feeling." Lord Courtland, who had been afraid of his son's levity, and had trembled lest Rollo, who had never been on very intimate terms with his brother, should show less sorrow than was becoming, was deeply satisfied. "How little we know what is in a man till he's tried," he said to his sister, Lady Beatrice. Lady Courtland, the mother of the young man, was happily long ago dead.

Thus, after setting out in the morning—full of tender ardour, notwithstanding his many doubts—to make the arrangements for his marriage, Rollo found himself at night one of the chief mourners in a house full of weeping. It was late at night when he got to his own room, and was able really to set himself to consider his own affairs. Which were his own affairs? The cares of the head of the family, the earl's heir and right hand—or those strangely different anxieties which had been in the mind of the second son? When he sat down to think it over, once more there came a giddiness and bewilderment over Rollo's being. He seemed scarcely able to force back upon himself the events which had happened at St. Michael's only this morning. The figure of Lottie appeared to him through the mist, far, far away, dimly apparent at the end of a long vista. Lottie. What had he intended to do? He had meant to get a license for his marriage to her, to arrange how he could get money—if money was to be had by hook or by crook—to see about the tickets for their journey, to decide where to go to—even to provide travelling-wraps for his bride. All this he had come to London to do only this morning, and now it almost cost him an effort to recollect what it was. He would have been glad to evade the subject, to feel that he had a right to rest after such a fatiguing day; but the revolution in and about him was such that he could not rest. St. Michael's and all its scenes passed before him like dissolving views, fading off into the mist, then rising again in spectral indistinctness. He could not think they belonged to him, or that the central figure in all these pictures was his own. Was it not rather his brother—he who had died? It seemed to Lord Ridsdale that he was settling Rollo's affairs for him, thinking what was best to be done. He had been horribly imprudent, and had planned a still greater imprudence to come, when death arrested him in mid-career; but, Heaven be praised, the heedless fellow had been stopped before he committed himself! Rollo shuddered to think what would have happened had the family been hampered by a wife. A wife! What a fool he had been; what a dream he had been absorbed in; folly, unmitigated, inexcusable; but, thank Heaven, he had been stopped in time. Lottie—that was her name, and she had been very fond of him; poor girl, it would be a great disappointment for her. Thus Rollo thought, not feeling that he had anything to do with it. It was all over, so completely over, that there was scarcely a struggle in his mind, scarcely any controversy with himself, on the subject. No advocate, heavenly or diabolical, spoke on Lottie's behalf. The whole affair was done with—it was impossible—there was no room even for consideration. For Lord Ridsdale to marry a nameless girl, the highest possibility in whose lot was to become a singer, and who had to be educated before even that was practicable, was not to be thought of. It was a bad thing for the poor girl; poor thing! no doubt it was hard upon her.

Thus—was it any doing of Rollo's? Providence itself opened a door of escape for him from his unwary folly. Law did not act in the same way; when good fortune came to him, by a mere savage and uncultivated sentiment of honour, he had gone to the girl who had been his sweetheart to propose that she should share it. Lord Ridsdale, however, was not of this vulgar strain. The savage virtues were not in his way—they were not possible in his circumstances. *Noblesse oblige*; he could not raise Lottie to the sublime elevation of the rank he had so unexpectedly fallen into. That was not possible. The matter was so clear that it barred all question. There was not a word to be said on her side.

Nevertheless, had it not been for all the trouble about poor Ridsdale's funeral, and the attentions required by the father, whose manner had so entirely changed to his surviving son, and who was now altogether dependent upon him—the new heir to the honours of the Courtland family might have broken off with his old love in a more considerate way. But he had no time to think. The very day had come before he could communicate with her; and then it had to be done abruptly. And, after all, a little more or less, what did it matter? The important point, for her sake especially, was that the change should be perfectly definite and clear. Poor Lottie! he was so sorry for her. It would be better, much better for her to hate him now, if she could; and, above all, it was the kindest thing to her to make the disruption distinct, beyond all possibility either of doubt or of hope.

CHAPTER XLII
"TILL FRIDAY"

Captain Despard put on his best coat after his return from the Abbey on the morning of Rollo's departure. He brushed his hat with more than his usual care; he found, after much investigation, among what he called his papers, an ancient and shabby card-case: and thus equipped set forth on his solemn mission. He had a bit of red geranium in his button-hole which looked cheerful against the damp and gloom of the morning. Polly, looking out after him, thought her Captain a finished gentleman, and felt a swell of pride expand her bosom—of pride and of anxiety as well—for if, by good fortune, the Captain should succeed in his mission, then Polly felt that there would be a reasonable chance of getting "her house to herself." Lottie's proud withdrawal from all the concerns of the house had indeed given her step-mother a great deal less trouble than she had expected; but she could not escape from the idea of Lottie's criticism; and the sight of the girl, sitting there, looking as if she knew better, though she never said anything, was to Polly as gall and wormwood. If she would have spoken, there would have been less harm. Mrs. Despard was always ready for a conflict of tongues, and knew that she was not likely to come off second best; but Lottie's silence exasperated her; and it was the highest object of her desires to get her house to herself. Lottie was coming down the Dean's Walk, calm, and relieved, and happy, after seeing her lover make his way down the Slopes, when the Captain turned towards the cloisters. Her heart gave a jump of irritation and excitement, followed by a gleam of angry pleasure. This mission, which was an insult to her and to Rollo alike, would be a failure, thank Heaven; but still it was a shame that it should ever have been undertaken. Oh, how unlike, she thought, the perfect trust and faith that was between them, to intrude this vulgar inquiry, this coarse interference, into the perfection of their love! It brought the tears to Lottie's eyes to think how ready he was to throw prudence to the winds for her sake, to accept all the risks of life rather than leave her to suffer; the only question between them being whether it was right for her to accept such a sacrifice. Lottie did not think of the approval of his family as she ought to have done, and as for the approval of her own, though the secret vexed her a little, yet she was glad to escape from the noisy congratulations to which she would have been subjected, and her father's unctuous satisfaction had her prospects been known. A few days longer, and the new wife whose presence was an offence to Lottie would have her house to herself. The two, upon such opposite sides, used the very same words; Lottie, too, was thankful above measure that Mrs. Despard would have her house to herself. She calculated the days—Wednesday, Thursday, Friday; Friday was the day on which she was to meet him, in the afternoon, while all the world at St. Michael's was at the afternoon service, and when the Signor, on the organ, which had been the accompaniment to all the story of their love, would be filling the wintry air with majestic and tender and solemn sound. She seemed to hear the pealing of that wonderful symphony, and Rollo's voice against it, like a figure standing out against a noble background, telling her all he had done, and when and how the crowning event of their story was to be. Her heart was beating loudly, yet softly, in Lottie's breast. Supreme expectation, yet satisfaction, an agitated calm, a pathetic happiness, feelings too exquisite in their kind to be without a touch of pain, filled all her being. The happiness she had most prized all her life was to have her ideal fulfilled in those she loved; and was it possible that any man could have more nobly done what a true lover should do, than Rollo was doing it? She was happy, in that he loved her above prudence and care and worldly advantage; but she was almost happier in that this generosity, this tender ardour, this quick and sudden action of the deliverer, was all that poet could have asked or imagination thought of. These were her fancies, poor girl; the fancies of a foolish, inexperienced creature, knowing nothing—and far enough from the truth that the charitable may forgive her, Heaven knows!

When she went in, Polly called her, with a certain imperiousness. She was on her way to her room, that sole bower of safety; but this Mrs. Despard had made up her mind not to allow. "You may show me those scales you were speaking of," said Polly. "I daresay I'll remember as soon as I see them. It will take up your attention, and it will take up my attention till your pa comes back. I'm that full of sympathy (though it can't be said as you deserve it), that though I have nothing to do with it, I am just as anxious as you are."

"I am not anxious," Lottie said proudly; but she would not condescend to say more. She brought out an old music-book with easy lessons for a beginner, at which she had herself laboured in her childhood, and placed it before her scholar. The notes were like Hebrew and Greek to Polly, and she could not twist her fingers into the proper places; these fingers were not like a child's pliable joints, and how to move each one separately was a problem which she could not master. She sat at the piano with the greatest seriousness, striking a note a minute, with much strain of the unaccustomed hand—and now and then looking up jealously to see if her instructress was laughing at her; but Lottie was too preoccupied to smile. She heard her father coming back in what she felt to be angry haste; and then, with her heart beating, listened to his step upon the stairs. At this Polly too was startled, and jumping up from her laborious exercise, snatched the old music-book from its place and opened it at random at another page.

"Me and Miss Lottie, we've been practising our duet," she said. "La, Harry! is that you back so soon?"

"The fellow's gone," said Captain Despard, throwing down his hat and cane; that hat which had been brushed for nothing, which had not even overawed Mr. Jeremie, who gazed at him superciliously, holding the Deanery door half open, and not impressed at all by the fine manners of the Chevalier. "The fellow's gone! He did not mean to go yesterday, that odious menial as good as confessed. He has heard I was coming, and he has fled. There could not be a worse sign. My poor child! Lottie!" said the Captain, suddenly catching a gleam of something like enjoyment in her eyes, "you do not mean to tell me that you were the traitor. You! Was it you told him? You may be a fool, but so great a fool as *that* couldn't be!"

Lottie scorned to deny what she had done. She was too proud and too rash to think that she was betraying herself by the acknowledgment. She met her father's eye with involuntary defiance. "You would not listen to me," she said, "and I could not bear it. It was a disgrace; it was humbling me to the dust. I warned him you were coming—" As she spoke she suddenly perceived all that was involved in the confession, and grew crimson-red, and then pale.

"So, miss," said Polly, "you're nicely caught. Keeping company all this time, and never to say a word to nobody; but if I were your pa, you shouldn't be let off like that. Was it for nothing but a bit of fun you've been going on with the gentleman? That's carrying it a deal too far, that is. And when your pa takes it in hand to bring him to the point, you ups and tells him, and frightens him away! I'd just like to know—and, Harry, I'd have you to ask her—what she means by it? What do you mean by it, miss? Do you mean to live on here for ever, and eat us out of house and home? If you won't work for your living, nor do anything to get an 'usband, I'd just like to know what you mean to do?"

"Hold your tongue," said her husband. "Let her alone. It is I that must speak. Lottie, is it really true that you have betrayed your father? You have separated yourself from me and put yourself on the side of a villain!"

"Mr. Ridsdale is not a villain," said Lottie, passionately. "What has he done? He has done nothing that can give you any right to interfere with him. I told him, because I would not have him interfered with. He has done nothing wrong."

"He has trifled with my child's affections," said the Captain. "He has filled our minds with false expectations. By Jove, he had better not come in the way of Harry Despard, if that's how he means to behave. I'll horsewhip the fellow—I'll kill him; I'll show him up, if he were twenty times the Dean's nephew. And you, girl, what can anyone say to you—never thinking of your own interest, or of what's to become of you, as Mrs. Despard says?"

"Her own interest!" cried Polly. "Oh, she'll take care of herself, never fear. She knows you won't turn her to the door, Harry. You're too soft, and they knows it. They'll hang upon you and eat up everything you have, till you have the courage to tell them as you won't put up with it. Oh, you needn't turn upon me, Miss Lottie. As long as there was a chance of a good 'usband I never said a word; but when you goes and throws your chance away out of wilful pride, then I'm bound to speak. Your poor pa has not a penny, and all that he has he wants for himself; and I want my house to myself, Harry; you always promised I was to have my house to myself. I don't want none of your grown-up daughters, as think themselves a deal better than me. I think I will go out of my mind with Miss Lottie's lessons, and Mr. Law's lessons, and all the rest. I never would have married you—you know I shouldn't—if I hadn't thought as I was to have my house to myself."

"My love," said the Captain, deprecatingly, "you know it is not my fault. You know that if I could I would give you everything. I had very good reason to think—"

"Papa," said Lottie, who had been standing by trembling, but less with fear than passionate disgust and anger, "do you agree in what she says?"

"Of course he agrees," says Polly. "He hasn't got any choice; he's obliged to say the same as me. He promised me when I married him as you shouldn't be long in my way. He told me as you was going to be married. One girl don't like another girl for everlasting in her road; and you never took no trouble to make yourself agreeable, not even about the music. Harry, do you hear me? Speak up, and say the truth for once. Tell her if she goes on going against me and you, and all we do for her, like this, that you won't have her here."

"My child," said the Captain, who, to do him justice, was by no means happy in his task, "you see me in a difficult position, a most difficult position. What can I say? Mrs. Despard is right. When I married it was my opinion that you, too, would soon make a happy and brilliant marriage. How far that influenced me I need not say. I thought you would be established yourself, and able to help your brother and—and even myself. I'm disappointed, I cannot deny it; and if you have now, instead of fulfilling my expectations, done your best, your very best, to balk—"

The Captain hesitated and faltered, and tried to swagger, but in vain. He had the traditions of a gentleman lingering about him, and Lottie was his child, when all was said. He could not look at her, or meet her eyes;

and Lottie, for her part, who could see nothing but from her own side of the question, who did not at all realise his, nor recognise any extenuating circumstances in the plea that he had thought her about to marry, so blazed upon him with lofty indignation as to have altogether consumed her father had he been weak enough to look at her. She did not even glance at Polly, who stood by, eager to rush into the fray.

"In that case," she said, with a passionate solemnity, "you shall be satisfied, papa. A few days and you shall be satisfied. I will not ask any shelter from you after—a few days."

Though it was happiness Lottie looked forward to, and there could no longer in this house be anything but pain and trouble for her, these words seemed to choke her. To leave her father's house thus; to make the greatest of changes in her life, thus; all Lottie's sense of what was fit and seemly was wounded beyond description. She turned away, listening to none of the questions which were showered upon her. "What did she mean? Where was she going? When did she intend to go? What was she thinking of?" To all these Lottie made no reply; she did not even wait to hear them, but swept away with something of the conscious stateliness of the injured, which it is so hard for youth to deny itself. Heaven knows her heart was full enough, yet there was in Lottie's deportment, as she swept out of the room, perhaps a touch of the injured heroine, a suggestion of a tragedy queen.

She went into her own room, where she found consolation very speedily in such preparations for her departure as she could make. She took out her white muslin dress, the simple garment which was so associated with thoughts of Rollo, and spent an hour of painful yet pleasant consideration over it, wondering how it could be made to serve for Saturday. Such a marriage made the toilette of a bride impossible; but Lottie could not bear the thought of standing by her lover's side, and pledging him her faith in her poor little brown frock which she had worn all the winter past. She thought that, carefully pinned up under her cloak, she might wear this, her only white gown, to be a little like a bride. It had been washed, but it had not suffered much. The folds might be a little stiffer and less flowing than before they had undergone the indignity of starch; but still they were fresh and white, and Lottie did not think it would be noticed that the dress was not new. Perhaps it was more appropriate that in her poverty and desolation she should go to him in the gown she had worn, not in one made new and lovely, as if there were people who cared. "Nobody cares," she said to herself, but without the usual depression which these words convey. She filled up the bodice of her little dress, which had been made open at the throat for evening use, and made it fit close. She put her pearl locket upon a bit of white ribbon. Doing this consoled her for the pangs she had borne. All the money she had of her own was one sovereign, which she had kept from the time of her mother's death as a last supreme resource in case of emergency; surely she might use it now. Taking this precious coin from the little old purse in which it was put away, in the deepest corner of an old Indian box, purse and box and coin all coming from her mother, Lottie went out to make a few purchases. She was forlorn, but her heart was light. She went down to the great shop not far from the Abbey gates, of which St. Michael's was proud, and bought some tulle and white ribbons. Poor child! her heart yearned for a little sprig of orange-blossom, but she did not venture to ask for anything that would betray her. It seemed to Lottie that she met everybody in the place as she went home with her little parcel in her hand. She met Mr. Ashford, for one, who was greatly surprised that she did not stop to speak to him about Law, and who was, indeed, to tell the truth, somewhat disappointed and chagrined that his liberality to his pupil had as yet met with no response except from that pupil himself. The Minor Canon looked at her wistfully; but Lottie, being full of her own thoughts, did nothing but smile in reply to his bow. Then she met Captain Temple, who, less shy, came to her side eagerly, complaining and upbraiding her that she had deserted him.

"I never see you," said the old man, "and my wife says the same, who takes so much interest in you. We hope, my dear," he said, kind yet half vexed with her, "that all is going better—going well now?"

"Indeed it is not, Captain Temple," Lottie said, tears coming suddenly to her eyes. She could not but wonder what he would think of her if he knew—if he would disapprove of her; and this sudden thought brought a look of anxiety and sudden emotion into her face.

"My poor child!" cried the old Chevalier. The ready moisture sprang to his eyes also. "Lottie," he said, "my wife takes a great interest in you; she would be very fond of you if she knew you better. Come to us, my dear, and we will take care of you." He said it with the fervour of uncertainty, for he was not sure, after all, how far he could calculate on his wife, and this gave a tremulous heat to his proposition.

But Lottie shook her head and smiled, though the tears were in her eyes. Oh, if she only dared to tell him what was the deliverance which was so near! He went with her to her door, repeating to her this offer of service.

"You might be like our own child," he said. "My wife cannot talk of it—but she would be very fond of you, my dear, when she knew you. If things go on badly, you will come to us?—say you will come to us, Lottie."

And while these words were in her ears, old Mrs. Dalrymple came out to her door, to ask if Lottie would not come in, if she would come to tea—if she would stay with them for a day or two.

"It is only next door, to be sure; but it would be a change," the old lady said. The ladies in the Lodges had forgiven her for her foolish pride, and for the notice the great people had taken of her, and for all the signs of discontent that Lottie had shown on her first coming to the Abbey. Now that the girl was in trouble they were all good to her, compassionate of her forlorn condition, and making common cause with her against the infliction of the stepmother, who was an insult to every one of them. There was not one Chevalier's wife who was not personally insulted, outraged in her most tender feelings, by the intrusion of Polly, and this quickened their sympathies to the poor girl, who was the most cruelly injured of all.

When Mrs. O'Shaughnessy saw the little group at her neighbour's door, she too came out. "It's her own fault, my dear lady, if she ever eats a meal there," said Mrs. O'Shaughnessy; "me and the Major, we are both as fond of her as if she was our own."

Lottie stood amongst them and cried softly, taking care that her tears did not drop upon the little parcel with the tulle, which was connected with still dearer hopes.

"I don't deserve that you should all be so good to me," she said. And indeed it was true; for Lottie had been very haughty in her time to the kind people who forgave her in her trouble.

Thus it was that she shared the dinner of the good O'Shaughnessys, and only went home in the afternoon, after Polly and the Captain had been seen to go out; when Lottie shut herself up in her room, and with much excitement began the "confection" for which she had bought the materials. It is needless to say that with so little money as she had ever had, Lottie had learnt, *tant bien que mal*, to make most of her own articles of apparel. How she had sighed to have her dresses come home all complete from the dressmaker's, like Augusta Huntington's! but as sighing did no good, Lottie had fitted herself with her gowns, and trimmed her little straw hats, and the occasional bonnet which she permitted herself for going to church in, since ever she was able to use her needle and her scissors. She had never, however, made anything so ambitious as the little tulle bonnet which she meant to be married in. She would have preferred a veil, could anyone doubt? but with no better tiring-room than the waiting-room at the railway, how was she to put herself into a veil? She had to give up that idea with a sigh. But, her pale cheeks glowing with two roses, and her blue eyes lighted up with the fires of invention, she sat all the afternoon, with her door locked, making that bonnet. If she but had a little sprig of orange-blossom to mark what it meant! but here Lottie's courage failed her. *That* she could not venture to buy.

In this way the days glided on till Friday came. Lottie packed up the things she cared for—the few books, the little trifling possessions of no value, which yet were dear to her to be removed afterwards, and put up her little bonnet (bonnets were worn very small, the fashion books said) in a tiny parcel which she could carry in her hand. Thus all her preparations were made. When she was not in her room making these last arrangements, she was out of doors—in the Abbey or on the Slopes—or with the friends who sought her so kindly, and gave her such meals as she would accept, and would have given her a great many more, overwhelmed her, indeed, with eating and drinking if she would have consented. To some of these Lottie allowed herself the privilege of saying that it was only for a few days she should remain in her father's house. She would not tell where she was going; to friends—yes, certainly to friends; but she would not say any more. This gave great relief to the minds of the Chevaliers generally, except to Captain Temple, who did not like it. The announcement even drew from him something like a reproach to his wife.

"If you had come forward—if you had gone to her when she was in trouble," he said, "we might have had a child again to comfort us." The old Captain was sadly put out, and did nothing but roam about all the day restless and lamenting. He went to the Signor's to hear what Lottie thought would be her last lesson, and thus bemoaned himself.

"Going away!" the Signor said in great surprise; and Lottie sang so well that day that the musician felt the desertion doubly. She sang fitfully but finely, saying to herself all the time, "To-morrow—to-morrow!" and taking her leave, as she supposed, joyfully, regretfully of Art. That day Lottie thought nothing whatever about Art. Her spirit was moved to its very depths. To-morrow the man whom she loved was coming to take her away from all that was petty, all that was unlovely in her life. From the hardness of fate, from the unkindness of her family, from the house that was desecrated, from the existence which was not made sweet by any love—he was coming to deliver her. The air was all excitement, all agitation, to Lottie. It was not so much that she was glad—happiness was in it, and trouble, and regret, and agitation, made up by all these together. It was life in its strongest strain, tingling, throbbing, at the highest pressure. The earth was elastic under her feet, the whole world was full of this which was about to happen; and how she sang! Those lessons of hers were as a drama to the Signor, but he did not understand this art. He had understood the struggle she made to get hold of her powers on the day when Rollo was not there, and Lottie had made a proud, forlorn attempt to devote herself to Song, as Song; he had understood the confusion and bewildered discouragement of the day when Mrs. Daventry assisted at the lesson; but this time the Signor was puzzled. There was nothing to excite her, only Mrs. O'Shaughnessy and Captain Temple, listeners who cared nothing for art, but only for Lottie; yet how she sang! He made her a little solemn compliment, almost for the first time.

"Miss Despard," he said, "you change from lesson to lesson—it is always another voice I hear; but this is the one I should like to retain; this is the one that shows what wonderful progress we have made."

Lottie smiled in a way which nearly won the Signor's steady heart. A golden dazzlement of light got into her eyes, as if the slanting afternoon sun was in them. She did not speak, but she gave him her hand—a thing which was very rare with Lottie. The Signor was flattered and touched; but he would not have been so flattered had he known that she was saying to herself, "It is the last time—it is the last!"

Mr. Ashford met the party coming out, and walked with them along the north side of the Abbey and through the cloisters. He could not make out why Lottie said nothing to him about her brother. To tell the truth, he wanted to have something for his money, and it did not seem that he was likely to get anything. He said to her at last, abruptly, "I hope you think Law is likely to do well, Miss Despard?"

"Law?" she said, looking up with wondering eyes.

He was so confounded by her look of bewilderment that he did not say anything more.

Next day dawned bright and fair, as it ought. A fair, clear, sunny winter's day—not a leaf, even of those few that hung upon the ends of the boughs, stirring—not a cloud. Earth in such a day seems hanging suspended in the bright sphere, not certain yet whether she will turn back again to the careless summer, or go through her winter spell of storm duty. Lottie had all her preparations made; her dress ready to put on in the morning; her little bonnet done up in a parcel incredibly small, a veil looped about it; and the great cloak, a homely waterproof, which was to cover her from head to foot, and conceal her finery, hung out all ready. Everything ready—nothing now to be done but to meet him on the Slopes, and to hear how all had been settled, and arrange for the final meeting on the wedding morning. Even her railway fare, so many shillings, was put ready. She would not let him pay even that for her until she belonged to him. She went out with the dreamy sweetness of the approaching climax in her eyes when the last rays of the sunset were catching all the Abbey pinnacles. She scarcely saw the path over which her light feet skimmed. The people who passed her glided like the people in a dream; the absorbing sweet agitation of happiness and fear, and hope and content, was in all her veins; her eyes were suffused with light as eyes get suffused with tears—an indescribable elation and alarm, sweet panic, yet calm, was in her breast. Mr. Ashford met her going along, swift and light, and with that air of abstraction from everything around her. She did not see him, nor anyone; but she remembered after, that she *had* seen him, and the very turn of the road where he made a half pause to speak to her, which she had not taken any notice of. In this soft rapture Lottie went to the corner of the bench under the elm-tree. It was too early, but she placed herself there to wait till he should come to her. This was the place where he was certain to come. By-and-by she would hear his step, skimming too, almost as light and quick as her own—or hear him vaulting over the low wall from the Deanery—or perhaps, to attract less notice, coming up the winding way from the Slopes. Where she sat was within reach of all the three. It was a little chilly now that the sun had gone down, but Lottie did not feel it. She sat down with a smile of happy anticipation on her face, hearing the Abbey bells in the clear frosty air, and then the bursting forth of the organ and all the strains of the music. These filled up her thoughts for the time, and it was not till the larger volume of sound of the voluntary put Lottie in mind of the length of time she had waited, that she woke up to think of the possibility that something might have detained her lover. It was strange that he should be so late. The light was waning, and the sounds about were eerie; the wind that had lain so still all day woke up, and wandered chilly among the bare shrubberies, tossing off the late leaves. She shivered a little with the cold and the waiting. Why did not he come? the hour of stillness was passing fast, the organ pealing, the light fading moment by moment. Why was not Rollo here?

At last there was a step. It was not light and quick like his step; but something might have happened to make it sound differently—something in the air, or something in him, some gravity of movement befitting the importance of the occasion. So anxiety beguiles itself, trying to believe what it wishes. The step came nearer, and Lottie roused herself, a little alarmed, wondering if anything (she could not tell what) could have happened to him—and looked round. A figure—a man coming her way—her heart jumped into her throat, then sank down, down, with a flutter of fright and pain. It was not Rollo—but what then? it might be only some chance passer-by, not having anything to do with her and him. Another moment, and she waited with an agonised hope that he was passing along without taking any notice, and that he had indeed nothing at all to do with her. But the steady step came on—nearer, nearer. She raised her head, she opened her eyes that had been veiled in such sweet dreams, with a wideness of fear and horror. What could he have to do with her? What had he come to tell her? The man came up to her straight, without any hesitation. He said, "Are you Miss Despard, ma'am? I was sent to give you this from my lord."

My lord—who was my lord? She took it with a gasp of terror. It was not Rollo that was my lord. The man, a middle-aged, respectable servant, gave her a look of grave pity and went away. Lottie sat still for a moment with the letter in her hand, thinking with wild impatience that the sound of those heavy departing steps would prevent her from hearing Rollo's light ones when he came. My lord—who was my lord? Suddenly an idea seized upon her. The light was almost gone. She tore the letter open, and read it by the faint chill shining of the skies, though it was almost too dark to see.

CHAPTER XLIII
THE END OF THE DREAM

Captain Temple was an old soldier, whose habit it was to get up very early in the morning. He said afterwards that he had never got up so early as on that morning, feeling a certain pride in it, as showing the magical power of sympathy and tenderness. He woke before it was light. It had been raining in the night, and the morning was veiled with showers; when the light came at last, it was white and misty. He was ready to go out before anyone was stirring. Not a soul, not even the milkman, was astir in the Dean's Walk. The blinds were still down over his neighbours' windows. The only one drawn up, he noticed in passing, was Lottie's. Was she too early, like himself? the question went through his mind as he passed. Poor child! her life was not a happy one. How different, he could not help feeling, how different his own girl would have been had she but been spared to them! He shook his white head, though he was all alone, wailing, almost remonstrating, with Providence. How strange that the blessing should be with those who did not know how to prize it, while those who did were left desolate! The Captain's step rang through the silent place. There was no one about; the Abbey stood up grey and still with the morning mists softly breaking from about it, and here and there, behind and around, smoke rose from some homely roof, betraying the first signs of waking life, Captain Temple walked briskly to the Slopes; it was his favourite walk. He made one or two turns up and down all the length of the level promenade, thinking about her—how often she had come with him here: but lately she had avoided him. He paused when he had made two or three turns, and leaned over the low parapet wall, looking down upon the misty landscape. The river ran swiftly at the foot of the hill, shewing in a pale gleam here and there. The bare branches of the trees were all jewelled coldly with drops of rain. It began to drizzle again as he stood gazing over the misty wet champaign in the stillness of the early morning. He was the only conscious tenant of this wide world of earth and sky. Smoke rising from the houses in the town, and a faint stir was beginning; but here on the hill there was no stir or waking movement, save only his own.

What was that? a sound—he turned round quickly—he could not tell what it was; was there someone about after all, someone else as early as himself? But he could see nobody. There was not a step nor a visible movement, but there was a sense of a human presence, a feeling of somebody near him. He turned round with an anxiety which he could not explain to himself. Why should he be anxious? but it pleased him afterwards to remember that all his sensations this morning were strange, uncalled for, beyond his own control. He peered anxiously about among the bushes and bare stems of the trees. At last it seemed to him that he saw something in the corner of the bench under the elm-tree. He turned that way, now with his old heart beating, but altogether unprepared for the piteous sight that met his eyes. She was so slim, so slight, her dress so heavy and clinging with the rain, that a careless passer-by might never have seen her. He hurried to the place with a little cry. Her head drooped upon the rough wooden back of the seat, her hands were wrapped in her cloak, nothing visible of her but a face as white as death, and wet—was it with rain or with tears? Her eyes were closed, her long dark eyelashes drooping over her cheek. But for her frightful paleness she would have looked like a child who had lost its way, and cried itself to sleep. "Lottie!" cried the old man; "Lottie!" But she made no response. She did not even open her eyes. Was she sleeping, or, good God—! He put his hand on her shoulder. "Lottie, Lottie, my dear child!" he cried into her ear. When after a while a deep sigh came from her breast, the old man could have wept for joy. She was living then. He thought for a moment what was to be done; some help seemed indispensable to him; then rushed away down through the cloisters to the house of Mr. Ashford, which was one of the nearest. The Minor Canon was coming downstairs; he had something to do which called him out early. He paused in some surprise at the sight of his visitor, but Captain Temple stopped the question on his lips. "Will you come with me?" he cried; "come with me—I want you," and caught him by the sleeve in his eagerness. Mr. Ashford felt that there was that in the old man's haggard face which would not bear questioning. He followed him, scarcely able in the fulness of his strength to keep up with the nervous steps of his guide. "God knows if she has been there all night," the Captain said. "I cannot get her to move. And now the whole place will be astir. If I could get her home before anybody knows! They have driven her out of her sweet senses," he said, gasping for breath as he hurried along. "I came for you because you are her friend, and I could trust you. Oh, why is a jewel like that given to those who do not prize it, Mr. Ashford, and taken from those that do? Why is it? why is it? they have broken her heart." The Minor Canon asked no questions; he felt that he too knew by instinct what it was. The rain had come on more heavily, small and soft, without any appearance of storm, but penetrating and continuous. The Captain hurried on to the corner where he had left her. Lottie had moved her head; she had been roused by his first appeal from the stupor into which she had fallen; her eyes were open, her mind slowly coming, if not to itself, at least to some consciousness of the external world and her place in it. The instinct that so seldom abandons a woman, that of concealing her misery, had begun to dawn in her—the first sign of returning life.

"Lottie, Lottie, my dear child, you must not sit here in the rain. Come, my pet, come. We have come to fetch you. Come to your mother, or at least to one who will be like a mother. Come, my poor dear, come home with me." The old man was almost sobbing as he took into his her cold hands.

Lottie did her best to respond. She attempted to smile, she attempted to speak mechanically. "Yes," she said, under her breath; "I will come—directly. It is—raining." Her voice was almost gone; it was all they could do to make out what she said.

"And here is a kind friend who will give you his arm, who will help you along," said Captain Temple. He stopped short—frightened by the change that came over her face; an awful look of hope, of wonder, woke in her eyes, which looked preternaturally large, luminous, and drowsy. She stirred in her seat, moving with a little moan of pain, and attempted to turn round to look behind her.

"Who is it?" she whispered. "Who is it? is it—you?"

Who did she expect it to be? Mr. Ashford, greatly moved, stepped forward quickly and raised her from her seat. It was no time for politeness. He drew her arm within his, not looking at her. "Support her," he said quickly to Captain Temple, "on the other side." The Minor Canon never looked at Lottie as he half carried her along that familiar way. He did not dare to spy into her secret, but he guessed at it. The hand which he drew through his arm held a letter. He knew none of the steps which had led to this, but he thought he knew what had happened. As for Captain Temple, he did not do much of his share of the work; he held her elbow with his trembling hand, and looked pitifully into her face, knowing nothing at all. "My poor dear," he said, "you shall not go back—you shall not be made miserable; you are mine now. I have found you, and I shall keep you, Lottie. It is not like a stepmother that my Mary will be. My love, we will say nothing about it, we will not blame anyone; but now you belong to me." What he said was as the babbling of a child to Lottie, and to the other who divined her; but they let him talk, and the old man seemed to himself to understand the position entirely. "They have driven her out of her senses," he said to his wife; "so far as I can see she has been out on the Slopes all night, sitting on that bench. She will be ill, she is sure to be ill—she is drenched to the skin. Think if it had been our own girl! But I will never let her go into the hands of those wretches again."

No one of the principal actors in this strange incident ever told the story, yet it was known all through the Abbey precincts in a few hours—with additions—that Captain Despard's new wife had driven her step-daughter out of the house by her ill-usage; turned her to the door, some said; and that the poor girl, distracted and solitary, had spent the night on the Slopes, in the cold, in the rain, and had been found there by Captain Temple. "When we were all in our comfortable beds," the good people cried with angry tears, and an indignation beyond words. Captain Despard came in from matins in a state of alarm indescribable, and besought his wife to keep indoors, not to allow herself to be seen. No one in the house had known of Lottie's absence during the night. She was supposed to be "sulky," as Polly called it, and shut up in her own room. When she did not appear at breakfast, indeed, there had been some surprise, and a slight consternation, but even then no very lively alarm. "She's gone off, as she said she would," Polly said, tossing her head; and the Captain had, though with some remorse and compunction, satisfied himself that it was only an escapade on Lottie's part, which would be explained by the post, or which Law would know about, or Mrs. O'Shaughnessy. Law had gone out early, before breakfast. It was natural to suppose he would know—or still more likely that his sister had gone with him, on some foolish walk, or other expedition. "I don't mean to hurt your feelings," Polly cried, "but I shouldn't break my heart, Harry, if they'd gone for good, and left us the house to ourselves." When Captain Despard came in from matins, however, the case was very different; he came in pale with shame and consternation, and ready to blame his wife for everything. "This is what has come of your nagging and your impudence," he said; and Polly flew to arms, as was natural, and there was a hot and dangerous encounter. The Captain went out, swearing and fuming, recommending her if she prized her own safety not to show herself out of doors. "You will be mobbed," he said; "and you will well deserve it."

"I'm going to put my hat on," said Polly, "and let them all see what a coward you are, as won't stand up for your wife." But when he had slammed the door emphatically after him, Polly sat down and had a good cry, and did not put on her hat. Oh, what a foolish thing it is, she repeated, to marry a man with grown-up children! It was nature, and not anything she had done, that was in fault.

Lottie made no resistance when she found herself in Mrs. Temple's care. To have her wet things taken off, to have a hundred cares lavished upon her, as she lay aching and miserable in the bed that had been prepared for her, soothed her at least, if they did nothing more. Chilled in every bit of her body, chilled to her heart, the sensation of warmth, when at last it stole over her, broke a little the stony front of her wretchedness. She never knew how she had passed that miserable night. The fabric of her happiness had fallen down on every side, and crushed her. Her heart had been so confident, her hopes so certain. She had not doubted, as women so often do, or even thought it within the compass of possibility that Rollo could fail her. How could she suppose it? and, when it came, she was crushed to the ground. The earth seemed to have opened under her feet; everything failed her when that one thing in which all her faith was placed failed. She had sat through the darkness, not able to think, conscious of nothing but misery, not aware how the time was passing, taking no note of the coming of the night, or of the bewildering chimes from the Abbey of hour after hour and quarter after quarter. Quarter or hour, what did it matter to her? what did she know of the hurrying, flying time, or its stupefying measures? It began to rain, and she did not care. She cared for nothing—not the cold, nor the dark, nor the whispering of the night wind among the bare branches, the mysterious noises of the night. The pillars of the earth, the arch of the sweet sky, had fallen. There was nothing in all the world but dismal failure and heart-break to Lottie. In the long vigil, even the cause of this horrible downfall seemed to fade out of her mind. The pain in her heart, the oppression of her brain, the failing of all things—hope, courage, faith—was all she was conscious of. Rollo—her thoughts avoided his name, as a man who is wounded shrinks from any touch; and at last everything had fallen into one stupor of misery. That it was the night which she was spending there, under the dark sky, just light enough to show the darker branches waving over it, the rain falling from it, Lottie was unconscious. She had nowhere to go, she had no wish to go anywhere; shelter was indifferent to her, and one place no more miserable than another. When Captain Temple roused her, there came vaguely to her mind a sense that her feelings must be hid, that she must try to be as other people, not betraying her own desolation; and this was the feeling that again woke feebly in her when Mrs. Temple took her place by the bedside where Lottie was lying. She tried to make some feeble excuse, an excuse which in the desperation of her mind did not sound so artificial as it was. "I give you a great deal of trouble," she faltered.

"Oh, my dear," said Mrs. Temple, with tears, "do not say so; let me do what I can for you—only trust in me, trust in me."

Lottie could not trust in anyone. She tried to smile. She was past all confidences, past all revelation of herself or her trouble. And thus she lay for days, every limb aching with the exposure, her breathing difficult, her breast throbbing, her heart beating, her voice gone.

Downstairs there was many an anxious talk over her between the three most intimately concerned. The old Captain held by his simple idea that she had been driven from home by her stepmother, that idea which all the Abbey had adopted. The Minor Canon was not of that opinion. He came every day to ask for the patient, and would sit and listen to all they could tell him, and to the Captain's tirades against Polly. "I think there was something more than that," he would say. And Mrs. Temple looked at him with a look of understanding. "I think so too," she said. Mrs. Temple had disengaged out of Lottie's cold hand the letter which she had been grasping unawares. She had not been able to resist looking at it, telling herself that she ought to know what was the cause. These two alone had any idea of it, and no one spoke to Lottie, nor did she speak to anyone of the cause of her vigil. She lay in a silent paradise of warmth and rest, cared for and watched at every turn she made, as she had never been in her life before. And by degrees the pain stole out of her limbs, her cough was got under, and the fever in her veins subdued. Of two things only Lottie did not mend. Her heart seemed dead in her bosom, and her voice was gone. She could neither sing any more, nor be happy any more; these are things which neither doctor nor nurse can touch, but for all the rest her natural health and strength soon triumphed. Her brain, which had tottered for a moment, righted itself and regained its force. She had no fever, though everybody expected it. She did not fall into "a decline," as was universally thought. She got better, but she did not get happy, nor did she recover her voice. When she was able to be brought downstairs, the good people who had taken her up made a little *fête* of her recovery. Mr. Ashford was asked to dinner, and the room was filled with flowers, rare hothouse flowers, on which the old Captain spent a great deal more than he could afford to spend. "To please the poor child, my dear," he said, apologetically; and Mrs. Temple had not a word to say. She winced still when in his simple way he would speak of "our own girl," but in her heart she made a kind of religion of Lottie, feeling sometimes, poor soul, as if she were thus heaping coals of fire, whatever they may be, upon the head—though it might be blasphemy to put it into words—of Him who had bereaved her. He had taken her child from her, and she had been angry, and perhaps had sinned in the bitterness of her grief; but now here was a child who was His—for are not all the helpless His?—whom she would not cast from her, whom she would take to her bosom and cherish, to show Him (was it?) that she was more tender than even the Father of all. "Thou hast taken mine from me, but I have not closed my heart to thine," was what, all unawares, the woman's heart said; for she was angry still, being a mother, and unable to see why she should have been bereaved.

A few days after Lottie had begun to be brought downstairs (for this was done without any will of hers), a visit was paid to her which had no small effect upon her life. She was seated in the invalid's place near the fire, a little table by her side with flowers on it, and a new book, and *Punch*, and the illustrated papers, all the little innocent *gâteries* of which the old Captain could think, the trifles which make the days of a happy convalescent sweet, and which Lottie tried hard to look as if she cared for; and with Mrs. Temple near her, watching her to see lest she should be too warm or too cold, lest she should want anything, with the anxious care of a mother. There was a prancing of horses outside the door, a tremendous knock, a rustle of silk, and wafting of perfume, and the door was opened and Mrs. Daventry announced. Augusta came in with a sweep which filled Mrs. Temple's little drawing-room. There did not seem room for its legitimate inmates in that redundant presence. Mrs. Temple ran to her patient, thinking Lottie was about to faint, but she recovered herself enough to smile faintly at Augusta when she spoke, which was as much as she did to anyone. Augusta seated herself opposite the convalescent, her train falling round her in heavy masses—the one all wealth and commotion and importance, the other so pale, so slight in her weakness, her brown merino dress hanging loosely upon her. Mrs. Temple was not made much account of by the fine lady, who made her a slight salutation, half bow, half curtsey, and took no further notice of "the people of the house."

"Well," she said, "how are you, and what has been the matter? There are the most extraordinary stories told about you. I have come to find out what is really the matter, Lottie. Mamma wishes to know too. You know you were always a kind of favourite with mamma."

"I will tell you about her illness," said Mrs. Temple. "She is scarcely well enough yet to enter into details."

"Oh," said Augusta, gazing blankly upon the "person of the house,"—then she returned to Lottie again. "I don't want you to enter into details; but they say the most extraordinary things; they say you were turned out of doors, and stayed all night on the Slopes—that, of course, can't be true—but I wish you would tell me what is true, that I may give the right version of the story. Mamma is quite anxious to know."

"Lottie, my dear, I will tell Mrs. Daventry," said Mrs. Temple, "it is too much for you;" and she held her point and recounted her little story with a primness which suited her voice and manner. Many were the demonstrations of impatience which the fine lady made, but it was not in her power to struggle against Mrs. Temple's determination. She turned to Lottie again as soon as the tale was told.

"Is that true? Only a very bad cold, and influenza from getting wet? Oh, we heard a great deal more than that; and your voice—we heard you had quite lost your voice. I promised the Signor to inquire. He is quite anxious, he always thought so much of your voice. He is an odd man," said Augusta, giving a blow in passing, "he thinks so differently from other people about many things. I promised to find out for him all about it. Have you really, really lost your voice, as everybody says?"

It was curious that Lottie, who had never been concerned about her voice, who had never cared anything about it, who had not wanted to be a singer at all, should feel, even in the midst of the greater and deeper unhappiness that possessed her, a distinct sting of pain as she heard this question. Her paleness was flushed with a sudden painful colour. She looked at Mrs. Temple wistfully again.

"You can hear that she is hoarse," said Mrs. Temple; "a very common consequence of a cold. She has lost her voice for the moment, but we hope to find it again."

"I think she must be dumb altogether, as she never answers me," said Augusta, fretfully. Then she tried another subject, with a triumphant certainty of success. "I don't know if you have heard of our trouble," she said, looking at her black dress. "You remember, Lottie, my cousin, Mr. Ridsdale? Oh, yes; you knew him a little, I think."

Once more Lottie's pale face flushed with painful overwhelming colour. She looked up with alarmed and troubled eyes.

"Oh, I see you remember him; he was such a flirt, he was always making himself agreeable to women. It did not matter who they were," said Augusta, fixing her eyes on her victim's face, "or what class of people, so long as they were at all nice-looking, or could sing, or draw, or anything. I remember I sent him out to try whether he could not hear you sing the very day I was married. He was another of the people who believed in you, Lottie. He did not hear you then, so he made mamma ask you, you remember. He had something to do with a new opera company, and he was always on the look-out for a new voice."

Once more Lottie turned her eyes upon Mrs. Temple, eyes full of anguish and wonder. Who else could she turn to?—not to the cruel executioner who sat opposite to her, with a lurking smile about her heartless mouth. How cruel a woman can be with a fair face, and no signs of the savage in her! Augusta saw that her arrow had struck home, and was encouraged to do more.

"Oh, yes; he was in a great state about your voice. He said it would make his fortune and yours too. He was always ridiculously sanguine. You know how he used to flatter you, Lottie, and go to all your lessons. Oh, you must not tell me that you don't remember, for I could see you liked it. Well," said Augusta, who did not lose a single change of colour, no quiver of her victim's lips, or flutter of her bosom, "that sort of thing is all over now. Oh, I daresay he will continue to take a great interest as an amateur; but his position is now entirely changed. My poor cousin Ridsdale, Rollo's eldest brother, was killed in the hunting-field about a fortnight ago. Such a shock for us all! but it has made a great change for Rollo. He is Lord Ridsdale now, and my uncle Courtland's heir. His servant came last Friday week to fetch some things he had left at the Deanery—for he had gone away for the day only, not knowing what had happened. Poor fellow; and yet, of course, though he was truly grieved and all that, it is great good fortune for him.

We are not likely *now*" Augusta added, with a faint smile, "to see much of him here."

Lottie did not say a word. She sat, no longer changing colour, perfectly pale, with the great blue eyes that had so expanded and dilated during her illness, fixed upon the vacant air. To hear him named was still something, and filled her with a sick excitement, an anguish of interest and agitation. After the long silence, after the cutting of all ties, after his cruel desertion of her, after the blow which had all but killed her, to hear of him had been something. Pain—yet a pain she was more eager to undergo than to meet any pleasure. But Lottie had not calculated upon the cruel, treacherous, yet careless, blow which fell upon her now, upon her quivering wounds. To hear her voice, was that what it was? not to see her because he loved her, but to hear her singing. Till now she had at least had her past. He was false, and had forsaken her, she knew, but once he had loved her; the Rollo who gazed up in the moonlight at her window had still been hers, though another Rollo had betrayed her trust and broken her heart. But now! the blood ebbed away from her face, and seemed to fail from her heart; the beating of it grew confused and muffled in her ears. She gazed with her great eyes, all strained and pained with gazing, at nothing. To hear her sing, not seeking her, but only running after a new voice! She sat with her hands clasped upon her lap in a kind of piteous appeal, and sometimes would look at the one and then the other, asking them—was it true, could it be true?

"I must go," said Augusta, having fired her shot, "and I am glad to have such a good account of you. Only a bad cold and a hoarseness, such as are quite common. Mamma will be pleased to hear, and so will the Signor. I can't tell him anything about your voice, because you have not let me hear it, Lottie. Oh, quite prudent—much the best thing not to use it at all; though with an old friend, to be sure—you look rather ill, I am bound to say."

Lottie sat still in the same attitude after this cruel visitor was gone, all her thoughts going back upon that time, which after all was only a few months, yet which seemed her life. She had given him up, or rather she had accepted his abandonment of her, without a struggle, without a hope; it had been to her as a doom out of Heaven. She had not even blamed him. It had killed her, she thought. She had not resisted, but it had killed her. Now, however, she could not submit. In her heart she fought wildly against this last, most cruel blow. He was not hers, he was cut off from her, by his own murderous hand; but to give up the lover who had loved her before he knew her, who had watched under her window and wiled her heart away, that she could not do. She fought against it passionately in her soul. The afternoon went on without a sound, nothing but the ashes softly falling from the fire, the soft movement of Mrs. Temple's arm as she worked; but the silence tingled all the time with the echo of Augusta's words, and with the hot conflict of recollections in her own heart, opposing and denying them. Mrs. Temple worked quietly by and watched, divining something of the struggle, though she did not know what it was. At last, all at once in the stillness, the girl broke forth passionately: "Oh, no, no," she cried, "not that! I will not believe it. Not that; it is not true."

"What is not true, dear? tell me," her companion said, laying down her work, and coming forward with tender hands outstretched, and pity in her eyes.

"You heard her," Lottie said, "you heard her. That it was to hear me singing—that it was all for my voice. No, no, not that! It could not be—*that* was not true. You could not believe *that* was true."

And Lottie looked at her piteously, clasping her hands, entreating her with those pathetic eyes for a little comfort. "Not that, not that," she said. "My singing, was it likely? Oh you cannot think *that*!" she cried.

Mrs. Temple did all she could to soothe her. "My poor child, it is all over—over and ended—what does it matter now?"

"It matters all the world to me," Lottie cried. Kind as her new guardian was, she could not understand that even when her happiness and her hopes were all crushed, it was a bitterness more exquisite, a sting the girl could not bear to believe that her foundations had been sand, that she had been deluded from the beginning, that the love she trusted in had never been. This sting was so keen and sharp that it woke her from the apathy of despair that was creeping over her. She was roused to struggle, to a passion of resistance and denial. "How can anyone but I know how it was? It all came from that; without that I should never have thought—we should never have met. It was the beginning. How can anyone know but me?" she cried, contending as against some adversary. When the first strain of this conflict was over, she turned, faltering, to her kind guardian. "I had a letter," she said; "it was *the* letter. I cannot find it." She gave her a look of entreaty which went to Mrs. Temple's heart.

"I have got your letter, Lottie. I have it in my desk, put away. No one has seen it. Let me put it into the fire."

"Ah, no! perhaps there may be something in it different from what I thought."

She held out her hands supplicating, and Mrs. Temple went to her desk and took out an envelope. Within was something all stained and blurred. The rain had half washed the cruel words away. Once for all, as Rollo's last act and deed, and suicidal exit from this history, the letter shall be copied here. Imagine how Lottie had been sitting, all happiness and soft agitation and excitement, waiting for him when this curt epistle came:—

"Dear Lottie,—

"An extraordinary change has happened in my life—not my doing, but that of Providence. It gives me new duties, and a new existence altogether. What we have been thinking of cannot be. It is impossible in every way. For me to do what I promised to you was, when we parted, a sacrifice which I was willing to make, but now is an impossibility. I am afraid you will feel this very much—and don't think I don't feel it; but it is an impossibility. I have things to do and a life to lead that makes it impossible. I hope soon someone will be raised up for you when you want it most, to give you the help and assistance I would so gladly have given. Could I but know that you assented to this, that you saw the reason for my conduct, I should be as happy as I now can ever be; and I hope that you will do so when you can look at it calmly. Farewell, dear Lottie, think of me with as little anger as you can, for it is not I, but Providence. Your voice will soon make you independent; it is only a momentary disappointment, I know, and I cannot help it. To do what we settled to do is now an impossibility—an impossibility. Dear Lottie, farewell!

"R. R."

Underneath, *Forgive me* was scrawled hastily, as if by an afterthought.

In the calm warm room, in the dull afternoon, under the eyes of her tender nurse, Lottie read over again this letter, which she had read with incredulous wonder, with stupefying misery, by the dim light of the evening under the black waving branches of the leafless trees. She gave a cry of anguish, of horror, of indignation and shame, and with trembling hands folded it up, and put it within its cover, and thrust it back into Mrs. Temple's keeping. "Oh, take it, take it," she cried wildly; "keep it, it has killed me. Perhaps—perhaps! the other is true too."

CHAPTER XLIV
APRÈS?

Law had been living a busy life at the time of this crisis and climax of his sister's existence. He had spent day after day in London, lost in that dangerous and unaccustomed delight of spending money, which is only tasted in its full flavour by those who are little accustomed to have any money to spend. Law was tempted by a hundred things which would have been no temptation at all to more experienced travellers—miracles of convenience and cheapness, calculated to smooth the path of the emigrant, but which were apt, on being bought, to turn out both worthless and expensive—and many a day the young fellow came home penitent and troubled, though he started every morning with an ever-renewed confidence in his own wisdom. Lottie's sudden illness had checked these preparations in mid-career. He had lost the ship in which he meant to have made his voyage and though he bore the delay with Christian resignation, it was hard to keep from thinking sometimes that Lottie could not have chosen a worse moment for being ill—a little later, or a little earlier, neither would have mattered half so much—but at the very moment when he was about to sail! However he allowed impartially that it was not his sister's fault, and did not deny her his sympathy. Law, however, had never been satisfied about the cause of her illness. He did not know why she should have sat out on the Slopes all night. Polly—he refused the idea that it was Polly. Mrs. Despard was bad enough, but not so bad as that; nor did Lottie care enough for the intruder to allow herself to be driven out in this way. But Law kept this conviction to himself, and outwardly accepted the story, not even asking any explanation from his sister. Whatever was the real reason, it was no doubt the same cause which kept her from listening to him when he had tried to tell her of the new step in his own career, and the unexpected liberality of the Minor Canon. "If it had but been he!" Law said to himself—for indeed he, who knew the value of money, never entertained any doubt as to Mr. Ashford's meaning in befriending him; he was a great deal more clear about this than Mr. Ashford himself.

He lost his passage by the ship with which he had originally intended to go. It was a great disappointment, but what could he do? He could not start off for the Antipodes when his sister might be dying. And as for his own affaīrs, they had not come to any satisfactory settlement. Instead of saying yes or no to his question to her, Emma, when he had seen her, had done everything a girl could do to make him change his intention. To make *him* change his intention!—the very idea of this filled him with fierce scorn. It was quite simple that she should make up her mind to leave everything she cared for, for love of him; but that he should change his purpose for love of her, was an idea so absurd that Law laughed at the simplicity of it. As well expect the Abbey tower to turn round with the wind as the weathercock did; but yet Law did not object to stroll down to the River Lane in the evenings, when he had nothing else to do, sometimes finding admission to the workroom when the mother was out of the way, demanding to know what was Emma's decision, and smiling at her entreaties. She cried, clasping her hands with much natural eloquence, while she tried to persuade him; but Law laughed.

"Are you coming with me?" he said—he gave no answer to the other suggestion—and by this time he had fully made up his mind that she did not mean to come, and was not very sorry. He had done his duty by her—he had not been false, nor separated himself from old friends when prosperity came; no one could say that of him. But still he was not sorry to make his start alone—to go out to the new world unencumbered. Nevertheless, though they both knew this was how it would end, it still amused Law in his unoccupied evenings to do his little love-making at the corner of the River Lane, by the light of the dull lamp, and it pleased Emma to be made love to. They availed themselves of this diversion of the moment, though it often led to trouble, and sometimes to tears; and Emma for her part suffered many scoldings in consequence. The game, it is to be supposed, was worth the candle, though it was nothing but a game after all.

On the day after Mrs. Daventry's visit, Lottie sent for her brother. He found her no longer a languid invalid, but with a fire of fervid energy in her eyes.

"Law," she said, "I want you to tell me what you are going to do. You told me once, and I did not pay any attention—I had other—other things in my mind. Tell me now, Law."

Then he told her all that had happened, and all he had been doing. "It was your sense, Lottie, after all," he said. "You were always the one that had the sense. Who would have thought when I went to old Ashford to be coached, that he would come forward like this, and set me up for life? Nor he wouldn't have done that much either," Law added, with a laugh, "but for you!"

"Law," cried Lottie, with that fire in her eyes, "this was what we wanted all the time, though we did not know it. It was always an office I was thinking of—and that I would be your housekeeper—your servant if we were too poor to keep a servant; but this is far better. Now we are free—we have only each other in the world. When must we go?"

"We!" cried Law, completely taken aback. He looked at her with dismay. "You don't mean you are coming? You don't suppose I—can take you."

"Yes," she cried, "yes," with strange vehemence. "Were we not always to be together? I never thought otherwise—that was always what I meant—until—"

"Ah," said Law, "that is just it—until! When you're very young," he continued, with great seriousness, "you think like that—yes, you think like that. A sister comes natural—you've always been used to her; but then, Lottie, you know as well as I do that don't last."

"Oh, yes—it lasts," cried Lottie: "other things come and go. You suppose you want something more—and then trouble comes, and you remember that there is nobody so near. Who could be so near? I know all you like and what is best for you, and we have always been together. Law, I have had things to make me unhappy—and I have no home, no place to live in."

"I thought," said Law, severely, "that they were very kind to you here."

"Kind! it is more than that," cried Lottie, her hot eyes moistening. "They are like—I do not know what they are like—like nothing but themselves; but I do not belong to them. What right have I to be here? and oh, Law, you don't know—. To walk about here again—to live, where one has almost died—to see the same things—the place—where it all happened—"

Lottie was stopped by the gasp of weeping that came into her throat. She ended with a low cry of passionate pain. "I must go somewhere. I cannot stay here. We will go together, and work together; and some time, perhaps—some time—we shall not be unhappy, Law."

"I am not unhappy now," said the young man. "I don't know why you should be so dismal. Many a fellow would give his ears to be in my place. But you—that's quite a different thing. A man can go to many a place where he can't drag his sister after him. Besides, you've got no outfit," cried Law, delighted to find so simple a reason, "and no money to get one. Old Ashford has been awfully kind; but I don't think it would be nice to draw him for an outfit for you. It wouldn't be kind," said Law, with a grin, "it would be like the engineer fellow in Shakespeare—burst with his own boiler. You know that would never do."

"A woman does not need an outfit, as a man does," said Lottie; "a woman can put up with anything. If you go away, what is to become of me? When you are young, whatever you may have had to make you unhappy, you cannot die when you please. That would be the easiest way of all—but it is not possible; you cannot die when you please."

"Die—who wants to die?" said Law. "Don't you know it's wicked to talk so. Why, there's your singing. You'll be able to make a great deal more money than I ever shall; and of course you may come over starring to Australia when you're a great singer; but it would be ruin to you now to go there. Don't be carried away by it because I'm lucky just now, because it's my turn," he said; "everybody wants to hold on by a fellow when he's in luck—but it is really you who are the lucky one of the family."

"My voice is gone," said Lottie, "my home is gone. I have nothing in the world but you. All I used to have a little hope in is over. There are only two of us in the world, brother and sister. What can I do but go with you? I have nobody but you."

"Oh, that's bosh," said Law, getting up from his seat in impatience. "I don't believe a word they say about your voice. You'll see it'll soon come back if you give it a chance; and as for having nobody but me, I never knew a girl that had so many friends—there's these old Temples, and heaps of people; and it seems to me you may marry whoever you like all round. A girl has no right to turn up her nose at that. Besides, what made old Ashford so kind to me? You don't find men doing that sort of thing for nothing in this world. I always think it's kindest to speak out plain," said Law, reddening, however, with a sense of cruelty, "not to take you in with pretending. Look here, Lottie. I can't take you with me. I have got no more than I shall want for myself, and I may have to knock about a great deal there before I get anything. And to tell the truth," said Law, reddening still more, "if I was to take a woman with me, it would be more natural to take—someone else. A fellow expects to marry, to make himself comfortable when he gets out there. Now you can't do that if you have a sister always dragging after you. I've told you this before, Lottie—you know I have. I don't want to hurt your feelings when you've been ill—but what can a fellow do? To say what you mean once for all, that is the best for both you and me."

Law made his exit abruptly when he had given forth this confession. He could say what was necessary boldly enough, but he did not like to face his sister's disappointment. It was a comfort to him to meet Mr. Ashford at the door.

"Lottie is upstairs," he said. "She wants me to take her with me, but I have told her I can't take her with me. I wish you would say a word to her."

Law rushed away with a secret chuckle when he had sent to his sister a new suitor to console her. If one lover proves unsatisfactory, what can be better than to replace him by another? Law felt himself bound in gratitude and honour to do all that he could for Mr. Ashford, who had been so kind to him; and was it not evidently the best thing—far the best thing for Lottie too?

The Minor Canon went upstairs with a little quickening of his pulse. He had been a great deal about Captain Temple's little house since the morning when he had brought Lottie there, and her name and the thought of her had been in his mind constantly. He had not defended himself against this preoccupation, for would it not have been churlish to put the poor girl out of his mind when she was so desolate, and had no other place belonging to her? Rather he had thrown open all his doors and taken in her poor pale image, and made a throne for her, deserted, helpless, abandoned as she was. A generous soul cannot take care of itself when a friend is in trouble. Mr. Ashford, who had been on the edge of the precipice, half consciously, for some time, holding himself back as he could, thinking as little about her as he could, now let himself go. He felt as the Quixotes of humanity are apt to feel, that nothing he could give her should be withheld now. If it did not do her any good, still it would be something—it was all he could do. He let himself go. He thought of her morning and night, cherishing her name in his heart. Poor Lottie—life and love had alike been traitors to her. "Though all men forsake thee, yet will not I," he said, as once was said rashly to a greater than man. What could he ever be to her, wrung as her heart was by another? but that did not matter. If it was any compensation to her, she should have his heart to do what she liked with. This was the sentiment in the mind of the Minor Canon, who ought, you will say, to have known better, but who never had been practical, as the reader knows. He went upstairs with his heart beating. How gladly he would have said a hundred words to her, and offered her all he had, to make up for the loss of that which she could not have. But what his generosity would have thrown at her feet, his delicacy forbade him to offer. Lottie, in her disappointment and desertion (which he only divined, yet was certain of) was sacred to him. Mrs. Temple was absent about her household concerns, and there was nobody in the drawing-room upstairs except Lottie, who in her excitement and despair did not hear his step, nor think that anyone might be coming. She was walking about the room, with her hands clasped and strained against her breast, her weak steps full of feverish energy, her eyes glowing with a fire of despair. "What shall I do? what shall I do?" she was moaning in the anguish of her heart.

When Ernest Ashford opened the door, her back was turned to him, so that he heard this moan, and saw the passionate misery of her struggle, before she knew that he was there. When she saw him a momentary gleam of anger came over her face; then she put force upon herself, and dropped her hands by her side like a culprit, and tried to receive him as she ought. As she ought—for was not he her brother's benefactor, whom all this time she had been neglecting, not thanking him as he had a right to be thanked? The change from that anguish and despair which she had been indulging when alone, to the sudden softening of courtesy and compunction and gratitude which, after a pathetic momentary interval of struggling with herself, came over her face, was one of those sudden variations which had transported Rollo in the beginning of their acquaintance by its power of expression. But this change, which would have pleased the other, went to the heart of the Minor Canon, to whom Lottie had never appeared in the light of an actress or singer, but only as herself.

"Mr. Ashford," she said faintly. "I wanted to see you—to thank you—"

She was trembling, and he came up to her tenderly—but with a tenderness that never betrayed its own character—grave and calm, for all that his heart was beating—and took her hand and arm into his, and led her to her chair. "You must not thank me for anything," he said.

"For Law—"

"No; not for Law. If it would give you any ease or any comfort, you should have everything I have. That is not saying much. You should have all I can do or think," he said, with a thrill in his voice, which was all that betrayed his emotion. "The misery of human things is that all I can do is not what you want, Lottie—and that what you want is out of my power."

He asked no permission to call her by her name; he was not aware he did it—nor was she.

"I want nothing," she said, with a passionate cry. "Oh, do not think I am so miserable and weak. I want nothing. Only, if Law could take me with him—take me away—to a new place—to a new life."

He sat down beside her, and softly pressed the hand which he held in his own. Yes, this was the misery of human things, as he said—he did not repeat the words, but they were in his face. That which she wanted was not for her, nor was his desire for him; other gifts might be thrown at their feet, and lie there unheeded, but not that for which they pined and were ready to die.

"Do you think it must not be?" she said. Lottie was willing to make him the judge of her fate—to allow him to decide for her how it was to be. Yes, but only in that way in which he was powerless. He smiled, with a sense of this irony, which is more tragic than any solemn verdict of fate.

"I do not think it could be," he said, "except with perfect consent and harmony; and Law—does not wish it. He is like the rest of us. He does not care for what he can have, though another man might give his life for it. I is the way of the world."

"I am used to it," said Lottie, bowing her head; "you need not say it i: the way of the world to break it to me, Mr. Ashford. Oh, how well I ought t know! I am used to being rejected. Papa, and Law, and—"

She put her hand over her hot eyes, but she did not mean to drop int self-pity. "Nobody cares to have me," she said after a moment, with th quiver of a smile on her lips. "I must make up my mind to it—and whe you are young you cannot die whenever you please. I must do somethin for myself."

"That is it," said the Minor Canon, bitterly—"always the same; betwee those you love and those that love you there is a great gulf; therefore yo must do something for yourself."

She looked at him wondering, with sad eyes. He was angry, but no with her—with life and fate; and Lottie did not blush as she divined hi secret. It was too serious for that. It was not her fault or his fault; neither o them had done it or could mend it. Had she but known! had he but know Now there was nothing to be done but to unite what little wisdom they ha over the emergency, and decide what she was to do—for herself. Her fathe had no place for her in his house. Law would not have her with him; he lover had forsaken her; and to those who would have had her, who woul have cherished her, there was no response in Lottie's heart. Yet here sh stood with her problem of existence in her hands, to be solved someho She looked piteously at the man who loved her, but was her friend abov all, silently asking that counsel of which she stood so much in need. Wha was she to do?

Just then the door opened, and Mrs. Temple came in with D Enderby, who had been kind to Lottie, as they all were, and who regulat everybody's health within the Precincts, from Lady Caroline downwar The good doctor, who had daughters of his own, looked with kind eye upon the girl, who was so much less happy than they. He took her slend wrist into his hand, and looked into her luminous, over-clear eyes, wet wit involuntary tears.

"She is looking a great deal better. She will soon be quite herself," h said cheerfully; but winked his own eyelids to throw off something, whic was involuntary too.

"Yes, yes," said Captain Temple, who had come in after him. "She wi soon be quite herself; but you must give her her orders to stay with u doctor. We want to be paid for nursing her—and now she will be able t run about on all our errands, and save us a great deal of trouble, and keep us happy with her pretty voice and her singing. Did you ever hear her sing, doctor? The Signor is very anxious about her. We must begin our lessons again, my pretty Lottie, as soon as ever the doctor gives leave."

Dr. Enderby looked very grave. "There is no hurry about that," he said, "let her have a little more time. The Signor must be content to wait."

Now Lottie had said, and they all had said, that her voice was gone; but when the doctor's face grew so grave, a cold chill struck to their hearts. She gave him a startled look of alarmed inquiry, she who had suddenly realised, now that all dreams were over, that question of existence which is the primitive question in this world. Before happiness, before love, before everything that makes life lovely, this mere ignoble foundation of a living, must come. When one is young, as Lottie said, one cannot die at one's own pleasure—and suddenly, just as she had got to realise that necessity, was it possible that this other loss was really coming too? She looked at him with anxious eyes, but he would not look at her, to give her any satisfaction; then she laid her hand softly on his arm.

"Doctor," she said, "tell me true—tell me the worst there is to tell. Shall I never have my voice again? is it gone, gone?"

"We must not ask such searching questions," said the doctor, with a smile. "We don't know anything about *never* in our profession. We know to-day, and perhaps to-morrow—something about them—but no more."

He tried to smile, feeling her gaze upon him, and made light of her question. But Lottie was not to be evaded. All the little colour there was ebbed out of her face.

"Shall I never sing again?" she said. "No—that is not what I mean; shall I never be able to sing as I did once? Is it over? Oh, Doctor, tell me the truth, is that over too?"

They were all surrounding him with anxious faces. The doctor got up hurriedly and told them he had an appointment. "Do not try to sing," he said, "my dear," patting her on the shoulder. "It will be better for you, for a long time, if you do not even try;" and before anyone could speak again he had escaped, and was hurrying away.

When he was gone, Lottie sat still, half stupefied, yet quivering with pain and the horror of a new discovery. She could not speak at first. She looked round upon them with trembling lips, and great tears in her eyes. Then all at once she slid down upon her knees at Mrs. Temple's feet.

"Now all is gone," she said, "all is gone—not even *that* is left. Take me for your servant instead of the one that is going away. I can work—I am not afraid to work. I know all the work of a house. Let me be your servant instead of the one who is going away."

"Oh, Lottie, hush, hush! are you not my child?" said Mrs. Temple, with a great outcry of weeping, clasping her shoulders and drawing the upturned face to her breast. But Lottie insisted gently and kept her position. In this thing at least she was not to be balked.

"Your servant," she said, "instead of the one that is going away. I am an honest girl, though they all cast me off. I cannot sing but I can work—your servant, or else I cannot be your child."

CHAPTER XLV
CONCLUSION

If this history had proposed to settle and bring to a dramatic conclusion even one single human life, the writer would falter here, feeling her task all unfulfilled; for what have we been able to do more than to bring our poor Lottie at the end of all things to a kind of dead-lock of all the possibilities of life? Such stoppages in the course of human affairs are, however, at least as common as a distinct climax or catastrophe. For one girl or boy whose life lies all fair before them after the first effort, how many are there who have to leave the chapter incomplete, and, turning their backs upon it, to try a second beginning, perhaps with less satisfaction, and certainly with a somewhat disturbed and broken hope! Lottie Despard had arrived at this point. Her love had not ended as happy loves end. It had been cut short by a cruel hand; her fabric of happiness had fallen to the ground; her visionary shelter, the house of her dreams, had crumbled about her, leaving nothing but bare walls and broken rafters. Her misery and dismay, the consternation of her young soul when, instead of that fair and pleasant future which was to be her resting-place, she found around her a miserable ruin, we have scarcely attempted to say. What words can tell such a convulsion and rending of earth and sky? She had believed in her lover, and in her love as something above the weakness of ordinary humanity. She had believed herself at last to have found in him the ideal after which she had sighed all her life. His generous ardour to help her whenever he found her in want of help, the enthusiasm of a love which she believed had been given at first sight, like the love the poets tell of, had filled Lottie's heart with all the sweetness of a perfect faith. Impossible to say how she had trusted in him, with what pure and perfect delight and approbation her soul had given itself up to him, glad beyond all expression not only to find him hers, but to have found him at all, the one man known to her for whom no excuse had to be made. The discovery that he was a traitor killed her morally—at least it seemed so to the poor girl when, all crushed and bleeding from a hundred wounds, she was taken to the house of her friends. But even that was scarcely a more horrible blow than the stroke administered delicately by Augusta while still the injured soul had not staunched its own bleeding or recovered from the first mortal overthrow. The earth that had been so solid opened round her in yawning mouths of hell, leaving no ground to stand upon. There was nothing that was not changed. She had not only lost her future, which was all happiness, and in which she had believed like a child; but she had lost her past. She had been deceived; or, worse still, she had deceived herself, seeking her own overthrow. The knowledge that it had not been love that brought Rollo under her window first, that it was altogether another sentiment, *business*, regard for his own interests—seemed to throw upon herself the blame of all that came after. Soul and heart, the girl writhed under the consciousness of having thus anticipated and brought on her fate. So vain, so foolish, so easily deceived, who was in fault but herself? Those thoughts gave her a false strength, or feverish impassioned power for a time. It was her own doing. She had been the deceiver of herself.

But who could deliver her from the dying pangs of love in her heart, those longings which are unquenchable, those protestations of nature against loss, those visions of excuses that might still be made, and suggestions of impossible explanation which in her mind she knew to be impossible even while her fancy framed them? Sometimes Lottie would find herself dreaming unawares that someone else, not Rollo, had written that cruel letter; that it was not by his will he had left her to bear the brunt of her disappointment under the elm-tree; that *it* was a forgery, and he detained by some act of cruel treachery and deceit. Sometimes a flood of passionate longing and yearning would sweep over her—a longing only to see him, to hear his voice, to ask why, why he could have been so cruel. Love does not die in a moment, nor does it come to a violent end when the object is proved unworthy, as some people think. With Lottie it was a lingering and painful conclusion, full of memories, full of relentings; the ground that had been gained by days of painful self-suppression being lost by one sudden burst of remembrance, the sight of something that brought up before her one of the scenes that were past.

While this process was going on wistful looks were directed to Lottie's lonely path by more than one spectator. The household of the Signor was deeply moved by the hapless fate of the young lady for whom young Purcell sighed with unavailing faithfulness. He could not be made to see that it was unavailing, and the Signor, blinded by his partiality for his pupil, did not or would not see it; and, as was natural, Mrs. Purcell could not understand the possibility of any girl being indifferent to John's devotion. She thought Lottie's troubles would indeed be at an end, and her future happiness secured, if her eyes were but opened to his excellence. So strong was this feeling in the mind of the family that the Signor himself took the matter in hand, and sallied forth with the anxious sympathy of all the household to put the case before Captain Temple, who was now recognised as Lottie's guardian. "In every country but England," the Signor said, "the friends arrange such matters. Surely it is much more judicious than the other way. There is some guarantee at least that it is not mere youthful folly. Now here is a young lady who is in very unfortunate circumstances, who has been obliged to leave her father's house—"

"I beg your pardon, Signor," said the Captain, trying hard to keep his temper, "but I do not think my house is a very bad exchange for Captain Despard's."

"Nobody who knows Captain Temple can have any doubt of that," the Signor said with a wave of his hand, "but what can her situation be in your house? You are not her relation. She has no claim, she has no right, nothing to depend upon; and if anything were to happen to you—"

"To be sure," said Captain Temple, with profound gravity, not untinctured with offence, "there is much to be said on that point. We are mortal like everybody else."

Explanations were not the Signor's strong point; he was wanting in tact everybody knew. "I am making a mess of it," he said, "as I always do. Captain Temple, you are a man of sense, you know that marriage is something more than a matter of sentiment. John Purcell is a very rising musician, there is nothing in our profession he may not hope for; he loves Miss Despard, and he could give her a home. Will you not recommend her to consider his suit, and be favourable to him? His origin perhaps is an objection—but he is a very good fellow, and he could provide for her."

Captain Temple kept his temper; he was always very proud of this afterwards. He bowed the Signor out, then came fuming upstairs to his wife. "Young Purcell!" he cried, "the housekeeper's son! as if all that was wanted was somebody to provide for her; but when a man has that taint of foreign notions," said the old Captain gravely, "nothing will wear it out."

Mrs. Temple did not respond as her husband would have wished. Indeed this was very often the case; she had not his quick impulses nor his ready speech. She said with a sigh, "I almost think the Signor is right. I wish we could do what he says. I know a man who is very fond of her, who would be very suitable, who would be sure to make her happy. I think if I could marry her to him I would take the responsibility; but she will not see it in the same light."

"Who is it? who is it?" Captain Temple said with lively curiosity. And when Mr. Ashford's name was mentioned to him, after some protestations of incredulity, he could find nothing to say but a fretful "Do you want to be rid of Lottie?" He for his part did not want to be rid of her. She was delightful to the old man. She walked with him and sat with him, and though she had not sufficiently recovered to talk much to him, yet she listened to him while he talked, which did almost as well. The old Chevalier was more happy than he had been since his own child married and went away from him. Why should Lottie be married and carried away from him too, for no better reason than that a man could provide for her? This indeed was the weak point in Captain Temples armour. He could not provide for his adopted daughter; but he was angry when this was suggested to him. He had got a new interest, a new pleasure in life, and he did not like the idea of dying and losing it. Why should not he live for years and keep the shelter of a father's roof over this girl, who was like his own?

As for the Minor Canon, it had only been when he took the girl home from her vigil on the Slopes that he allowed himself fully to confess the state of his feelings towards her. When he had drawn her hand within his arm and felt her light weight upon him, holding up by close clasping of his own, the soft arm which he held, the floodgates had opened. He knew very well by instinct and by observation that Lottie loved, not him, but another man. He felt very sure that what had happened had little to do with her stepmother but a great deal to do with her lover; and yet at that very moment, the most discouraging and hopeless, those gates opened and the stream flowed forth, and he no longer attempted any disguise either with himself or with Mrs. Temple, who saw through and through him. Law, whom nobody supposed to have any discrimination, had seen through and through him long ago. Law felt that it was not at all likely that any man would sacrifice so much money and trouble on *his* account; and indeed from the beginning of their acquaintance he had read in "old Ashford's" eye an expression of weakness of which the astute youth was very willing to take advantage. When, however, Mr. Ashford himself gained this point of making no further resistance, and attempting no further concealment the acknowledgment to himself of the new sentiment, little hopeful as it was, had brought him a sense of happiness and freedom. Love in his heart was sweet, even though it had no return. It made life other than it had ever been. It opened possibilities which to the middle-aged Minor Canon had all been closed before. Handel may be a consolation or even a delight; and pupils, though neither consolatory nor delightful, at least keep a man from the sense that his life is useless; but neither of these things make up the sum of human requirements, nor do they help to reveal the *fin mot* of that mortal enigma which is more hard to solve than all the knots of philosophy. It seemed to Mr. Ashford when he gave up all resistance, and let this flood of tenderness for one creature take possession of his heart, that a sudden illumination had been given to him, a light that cleared up many difficult matters, and made the whole world more clear. With this lantern in his hand he thought he might even go back to tread the darker ways of the world with more fortitude and calm. The miseries of the poor seemed to him more bearable, the burdens of humanity less overwhelming. Why? but he could not have told why. Perhaps because life itself was more worth having, more beautiful, more divine with love in it; a poor man, though he was starving could not be so poor with that to keep him alive. He remembered in his early experiences, when he had fled from the horrible mystery of want and pain, to have seen that other presence which then he took no note of, in the poorest places—gleaming in the eyes of a woman, in a man's rough face, which knew no other enlightenment. This, then, was what it was. In the sweetness of the heavenly discovery perhaps he went too far, and felt in it the interpretation and compensation of all. Naturally, a man who has found a new happiness does exalt it above the dimensions of any human possession. It made the Minor Canon feel his own life too sheltered and peaceful, it made of him a man among other men. It seemed to him now that he wanted to go and help his brothers who were suffering, whose suffering had appalled him, from whom he had fled in excess of pity.

But he did not say one word of his love to Lottie, except those vague words which have been recorded. What was the use? She knew it as he knew it; and what could it matter? After the first impulse of speech, which was for her sake rather than his—to comfort her wounded pride, her sense of humiliation, if nothing else, by the knowledge that she was priceless to another if rejected by one—no desire to speak was in his mind. He surrounded her with every care he was permitted to give, with a thousand unexpressed tendernesses, with a kind of ideal worship, such as was most likely to soothe her wounds and to please her, at least, with a sense that she was beloved. In this way the winter went slowly on. Law did not sail till the early spring, being detained by the Minor Canon as he would, if he could, have detained a ray of sunshine that warmed her. And thus Lottie was surrounded by all the fairest semblances of life.

The fairest semblances! How often they collect about those who can derive no advantage from them! A good man loved her, but Lottie could not accept his love; the kindest domestic shelter was given to her, but she had no right to it—she was not the daughter of these kind people, and they would not make her their servant as she had asked them to do. Musing in her own mind over all that lay about her, this seemed the only true standing ground that she could hope for. Now that she wanted a way of living, a real occupation, her voice had failed her and she could not sing; now that she had the doors of marriage opened before her, her heart was too sick even to contemplate that possibility; now that she had a home where she was beloved, it was not her home but the house of a stranger. To all this she had no right. If they would let her be their servant, that would be true; if Mr. Ashford would see that she was not worth loving, that would be true; if she could take up the trade she had despised, in that there would be an honest refuge. All these things were out of her reach. She said nothing about the thoughts in her heart, but they burned within her; and nobody understood them, except perhaps Mr. Ashford, to whom she never confided them. Law thought her very well off indeed, and declared frankly that he would leave England with an easy mind: "You are one that will always fall on your feet," he said, with perfect satisfaction. Captain Despard even, who had at first resented the new arrangement of affairs, came at last in his finest manner and made very pretty speeches to Captain Temple and his wife. "If, as I understand, my daughter's society is a real pleasure to you," he said, "I am always glad when I or mine can be of use to my neighbours, and certainly, my dear Madam, she shall stay. Indeed, in the present state of my domestic circumstances," he added, with a wave of his hand, not perceiving Captain Temple's angry eagerness to speak, which his wife subdued with a supplicating gesture, "I will not conceal from you that it is an ease to my mind to know that Lottie is among the friends of her own choice. My wife and she," Captain Despard said, with a little shrug of his shoulders—"we all know what ladies are, and that occasionally unpleasantnesses will occur—my wife and she have not got on together." Thus Lottie was left by those who belonged to her. And when she retired to the room that was her own in the new home—which was so like the little room in the old, but so much more dainty, with everything in it that the old people could think of to make her comfortable, and all the little decorations which a mother invents for her child, Lottie would stand in the midst of these evidences of love and kindness, and ask herself what she could do—she had never been so well off in her life, what could she do? She had "no claim" upon the Temples, as the Signor said, "no right" to their kindness. The Captain's niece, who lived in St. Michael's, looked at the interloper, as the nearest relative of a foolish old couple who were wasting their means upon a stranger might be excused for looking. What was she doing but living on their charity? What could she do? Oh, that she had now the voice which she had cared so little for when she had it! How strange, how strange it all seemed to her now! She had, she said to herself, a trade, an honest trade in her hands, and she had not cared for it, had struggled against its exercise, had not wished to qualify herself for its use; and now it was lost to her. This was the only thing that was Lottie's fault; the other strange paradoxes about her had come without any doing of hers. But the result of all was that, with love and kindness on every side, she had no place that belonged to her, no right to anything. After the kind people who were so good to her had gone to their rest, the girl would sit and think over this problem. What was she to do? To be obliged to think of this did her good; it took her mind away from the wounds of her heart, it brought in new objects—new thoughts. She could not dwell for ever, as a disengaged mind might have done, amid the ruined temples and palaces of her love; she could not sink to the ground, and conclude, as in happier circumstances a broken-hearted girl might have been tempted to do, that all was over. On the contrary, life not being over, nor any end procurable by means of hers, an entire world of new difficulties and troubles was brought in which Lottie had to meet, and, as she might, find a solution for.

On the day before Law's departure, which had been so often delayed, she went back to her father's house, under her brother's guardianship, to take away the few little possessions which remained there. Law had been a very faithful guardian of Lottie's little belongings. There was nothing that Polly would have liked better than to enter and rummage through her step-daughter's things, searching for secrets through all the little drawers and boxes which Lottie had taken a girlish pleasure in keeping in good order. But Law had stood up like a dragon for his sister's property; and Captain Despard, who sometimes put himself on Lottie's side, by a certain *esprit de famille* against the wife, who, after all, was an alien and not one of them, supported Law. Thus the men of her family, though they had not hesitated to treat her carelessly and even harshly themselves, yet made a certain stand against the interference of any other. It was a day in early April when Lottie reluctantly went into her father's house on this errand. Polly was out; the house was vacant and quiet as when it had been her own, and it is not to be described with what a yearning the girl looked at the shabby furniture, the old piano, the faded rooms in which she had spent many a troubled and many a dull day, and beat her wings against the bars of her cage, and wished for a hundred things which were never to be hers. The reader knows how far Lottie had been from being happy: but yet she thought she had been happy, and that nothing better could have been desired than to be the household Providence, and "take care," as she called it, of her father and brother. All that was over. She could not bear to go into the little drawing-room, where he had visited her, where she had lived in such a world of dreams. Her heart beat as she went up the old stairs. She was far better off with the Temples, who could not pet or serve her enough; yet with what a yearning she came into the house which had once been hers, but in which now there was no place for her! In her own room, thanks to Law's care, she found everything as she had left it; and it is not to be told what anguish filled Lottie's breast as she looked at her little white dress, all carefully prepared for the event which was never to happen, and the little box with the bonnet which she had made in such sweet agitation and tumult of heart. And there was the pearl locket upon its white ribbon, her sole ornament. She gathered these things together and carried them, not letting even Law touch them, to her new home. She could not speak as she went up and shut herself in her room. A little fire was burning there, a luxury unknown to Lottie in the days when she was her own mistress, and no one cared how chilly she might be. Then with old Lear's "climbing sorrow" in her throat, she undid the little bit of maidenly finery for which she had so much wanted a sprig of orange blossom. It was a nothing, a little knot of tulle and ribbon—a piece of vanity not worthy a thought; so any moralist would have said who had seen Lottie stand speechless, tearless, a great sob in her throat, with the poor little bonnet in her hand. A bonnet, there is nothing tragic in that. She put it upon her fire and watched the light stuff flame and fall into sudden ashes. It was the affair of a moment; but those hopes, those prospects of which it had been the token, her life itself, with all that was beautiful in it, seemed ended too.

Then she sat down for the hundredth time and confronted the waste of darkness that was her life. What was she to do? Perhaps it was the final ending of her dream, symbolised by the destruction of that bit of tulle and ribbon, which moved her. For the first time her dreamy self-questions took a different tone. She asked herself, not what am I to do? but something more definite. Law was going away the next day, the only being except her father to whom she had any right, on whom she had any claim—going away in comfort, in high hope, as much as she could have desired for him. By whose doing? She had given up the care of Law, selfishly absorbed in her own hopes; and who was it who had taken her place and done the thing which Lottie had only wished and longed to do? She seemed to see him standing before her, with tenderness beyond words in his eyes. Always her good angel: how often he had interposed to help her!—from that early time at the Deanery when she had sung false in her agitation, and he had covered the error and beguiled her into the divine song which at that very moment she could hear thrilling all the air, pealing from the Abbey. Was it because this happened to be the afternoon anthem that she thought of that simple beginning of the Minor Canon's benefits? Never since had he failed her; though of all the people upon whom Lottie had no claim, he it was on whom she had the least claim. He had saved Law from his aimless idleness, and it was he who had awakened herself out of the miserable dream that had almost cost her her life. How could she repay him for all he had done for her? In one way, one only way. She shuddered, then stilled herself, and faced the thought with all the courage she had left. Marry him! If he would have her, if he wanted her, why should not she marry him? She trembled as the words came into her mind. It was not she that said them; something seemed to say them in her mind, without any will of hers. So good a man, so kind. Did it matter so much whether she liked it, whether she did not like it, so long as it pleased him? Perhaps this was not the right way in which such a calculation ought to be made, but Lottie did not think of that. At all times it had been easier for her to think of others than of herself. Only once had she pleased herself, and no good had come of it. Her heart began to beat with a heroic impulse. She was not worth his having, she whom everyone had cast off; but if he thought so? She shuddered, yet her heart rose high in her bosom. She would do her best, she would be a good wife, that would be within her power. She would serve him humbly, that he might forgive her for not loving him. She rose up to her feet unconsciously as this great resolution came upon her mind.

"Lottie," said Law at her door, "the service is over, and the Signor is practising. Come over to the Abbey with me. I'd like to wander about the old place a little the last night I am here. Come, it'll be something to think of," said Law, more moved than he liked to show, "when we're thousands of miles separate over the sea."

Lottie did not wait to be asked again. She hurried to him, glad to be thus delivered from the thoughts that were getting too much for her. Long, long months had passed since the brother and sister had gone to church together, their close vicinity to the Abbey and its frequent services had broken up the old childish Sunday habits. And it was not going to church in the ordinary way, but only roaming through to the silent beautiful place all deserted, with the organ pealing through its silence. Law's heart was touched, though he was too successful and prosperous now to be easily moved. He strayed about the majestic stillness of the nave with tears in his eyes, thinking—this time to-morrow! This time to-morrow he would probably be prosaically ill or prosaically comfortable, and thinking little of what he left. But for the moment it seemed to Law that when he once was gone, his heart would turn like that of any poet, to the sweet friends to whom that day he had said farewell.

The Abbey was altogether still except for the music. No one was about; the last ray of the westerly sun had got in among the canopy work over the stalls, and tangled itself there. Underneath the shadows of the evening were creeping dimly, and through the great vault the organ pealed. What bursts of wonderful sound, what glories in the highest, what quiverings of praise unspeakable! Lottie raised her face unawares to the gallery from which that music came. How her life had gone along with it, shaping itself to that high accompaniment! It had run through everything, delight and misery alike, good and evil. Her heart was moved already, and trembling under the touch of new impulses, resolutions, emotions. She stood still unawares, with her face turned that way, a new light coming upon it; once more the music got into her soul. With her head raised, her arms falling by her side, her heart going upwards in an ecstasy of sudden feeling, she stood spell-bound. She did not hear—how should she?—a whisper in the organ-loft, a noiseless change of music, nor see the anxious faces looking out upon her from among the fretwork of the carved screen. The torrent of sound changed; it breathed into a celestial softness of sorrow and hope; tears dropped liquid like a falling of rain; a counter stream of melody burst forth. Lottie did not know what she was doing, the spell upon her was broken. "I know that my Redeemer liveth:" she lifted up her voice and sang.

In the organ loft there was a group which clustered together, scarcely venturing to breathe. The Signor was the one who had most command of himself. "I always knew it would come back," he said in sharp staccato syllables, as he played on. Young Purcell, who loved her, sat down in the shadow and laughed and cried, blubbering not with dignity. The Minor Canon, who did not once take his eyes from her, waiting the moment that she might falter or want succour, watched, looking over the carved rail with face lighted up like her own.

Thus was Lottie restored to Art; was it to Love too?